THE ADVENTURES
OF MR. CLACKWORTHY

WILDSIDE PULP CLASSICS

THE ADVENTURES OF MR. CLACKWORTHY

CHRISTOPHER B. BOOTH

INTRODUCTION BY STEVE LEWIS

WILDSIDE PRESS

THE ADVENTURES OF MR. CLACKWORTHY

An original publication of Wildside Press.
www.wildsidepress.com

CONTENTS

MR. CLACKWORTHY: AN INTRODUCTION

There are very few people around today who might be considered experts on the life and fortunes of Mr. Amos Clackworthy, whose adventures you are about to read in this collection, but on the basis of doing a little research on the net and elsewhere, perhaps I could be counted among them. His stories, about 50 of them in all, appeared in the pages of Street & Smith's *Detective Story Magazine* back in the 1920s and 1930s. Two collections of these stories appeared in hardcover, about which more later.

What I know about the author, Christopher B. Booth, is that he was a prolific writer for the pulp magazines, with just under three and a half pages of entries in Cook and Miller's massive index of the detective pulps, *Mystery, Detective, and Espionage Fiction*, the work you absolutely must have if you are a collector or researcher of pulp magazines, rather than only a reader.

These are only the detective stories. On Bill Contento's FictionMags website[1], you can also find a smattering of western stories for him, and I know these are only the tip of the iceberg, as relatively few of the western magazines have been indexed yet.

According to Al Hubin's *Crime Fiction IV*, Booth wrote ten novels under his own name, all from Chelsea House, and eight more as by John Jay Chichester, also all from Chelsea House. Also to his credit is one book on which he shared the writing duties, and that was with Isabel Ostrander, another long-time writer for the pulps.

To point out that you can not always trust the Internet for factual information, some sites suggest that Christopher B. Booth was a pseudonym for Isabel Ostrander. Not so, even

[1]   http://users.ev1.net/~homeville/fictionmag/0start.htm

though Ostrander (who died in 1924) really was the lady behind 'Robert Orr Chipperfield,' 'David Fox,' and 'Douglas Grant.'

Chelsea House was the hardcover publishing arm of Street & Smith Publications, which also produced *Detective Story Magazine*, where most if not all of the novels it published were serialized first.

Or cobbled together out of short stories, as was *Mr. Clackworthy* (Chelsea House, 1925), the first collection of his adventures. The second volume, *Mr. Clackworthy, Con Man* (Chelsea House, 1927) was produced the same way.

How much overlap there is between those books and this, I do not know, but it is more than likely that there will be some. The truth is that neither book is easy to find. Better that you have this one than you burden yourself with locating either of the two earlier ones.

Enough of the general background. If you did not know before (but if you were paying close attention, you will know now), Mr. Clackworthy was one of those protagonists so often on the wrong side of the law in the 1920s, a con man. I imagine someone could write a thesis if not a dissertation on such individuals in the world of crime fiction.

Here is an off-the-wall question. What fictional character would qualify as the last in the line of con men, preying mostly on the rich and unscrupulous, but not necessarily giving to the poor, of which Mr. Clackworthy does not make a general practice?

This is not a question for which I have an answer, nor will I even attempt to list any other characters who fall into the category. If you can help, please do, otherwise we shall leave the matter to someone who needs a thesis if not a dissertation on their academic record. (Of course such a someone then would be also obliged to put into perspective *why* con men who preyed mostly on the rich and unscrupulous were so prevalent in the 1920s. One can guess, however.)

As a start to such a project, it belatedly occurs to me, if you will allow such an interjection, may be *Yesterday's Faces #3: From the Dark Side*, by Robert Sampson (Bowling Green Press, 1987), a rollicking account of all sorts of bad guys who inhabited the pages of the pulp magazines.

And by the way, before it slips my mind and we head off into more specific commentary, I would like to point out that in the pages of *Detective Story Magazine* Mr. Clackworthy met another of that magazine's regular characters, Johnston McCulley's lisping pickpocket, Thubway Tham: "Mr. Clackworthy and Thubway Tham" (*Detective Story Magazine*, March 4, 1922). Even though Cook-Miller suggests that only Booth was the author, this may be the first team-up on record between two characters created by separate authors. (Does one count, however, *Arsene Lupin Versus Holmlock Shears*, by Maurice LeBlanc [Richards, 1909]? One must posit some ground rules, one supposes.)

Further investigation into the subject reveals another story of interest: "Thubway Tham and Mr. Clackworthy," by Johnston McCulley (*Detective Story Magazine*, February 18, 1922, or two issues earlier). You can read this story in the recent edition of Tham thtories published by Wildside Press, *Tales of Thubway Tham*, although in the Wildside edition the story is retitled "Thubway Tham Meets Mr. Clackworthy."

One source suggests that the team-up was a three-part serial. This may be so, but if indeed it is, I have not yet uncovered a third tale in the triptych, and to this date, the matter rests, at least for now.

Let's get on with things. The best way to do that, I decided the moment I started reading it, is to quote the opening paragraphs of the first story in the first Chelsea House collection, right from the beginning:

"The greed of the human heart!" Mr. Amos Clackworthy, confidence man deluxe, sighed as he laid down his newspaper, which was folded to the want ad pages. He had been for some time engrossed in an analytical perusal of the "Business Chances" column.

James Early, whose record at police headquarters credited him with the alias of "The Early Bird," was standing at the window of Mr. Clackworthy's [Chicago] Sheridan Road apartment, gazing glumly at the stream of traffic that flowed past in its usual Sunday afternoon flood. The Early Bird was a lost soul during those times when there was none of Mr. Clackworthy's nefarious schemes under way to occupy his mind and to keep his wits sharpened.

All con men naturally work on the concept of greed, as many a Nigerian knows full well today. Booth's prose style is not dissimilar to that of his contemporary (at the time), Erle Stanley Gardner, whose Lester Leith stories for *Detective Fiction Weekly* started out in very much the same fashion.

Most of Mr. Clackworthy's victims well deserve it — greedy bankers, swindlers, unscrupulous investors, and so on — getting their comeuppance in a rough-and-tumble sort of justice, in a naïve, twinkle-in-the-eye sort of way, but even innocent banks sometimes fell afoul of his various and sundry plots and plans. (But were banks truly innocent of wrongdoing in the 1920s? Perhaps Booth's readers did not really think so.)

In any case, these works were written, read and enjoyed in a different time and place. If you've made it this far into this introduction, however, I see no reason why you shouldn't read and enjoy the Amos Clackworthy stories, too, even if no one is writing them like this any more.

— Steve Lewis
January, 2006

MR. CLACKWORTHY TELLS THE TRUTH

Mr. Amos Clackworthy, glancing up from a sheaf of papers which littered the rosewood table in the center of the big living room, smiled. Tilting back in his chair, he lighted one of his expensive cigars, and waited for the outraged monologue which he knew was to follow. It was given without invitation.

"Eighteen seeds for these kicks yesterday — and look at 'em!" exploded James Early. "Cast an eye on 'em; look like they'd been in a battle royal with a couple of hayrakes. You'd think I'd been tryin' to kick down th' door of th' sub-treasury."

"Let me try my hand at deduction, James," chuckled Mr. Clackworthy. "My first guess would be that you have ridden home on a surface car during the rush hour."

"Yeah," agreed The Early Bird sourly, "all th' strap-hangers must wear iron cleats on their gunboats; a sardine can is a forty-acre field alongside them street snails."

Mr. Clackworthy nodded gravely.

"Sit down, James. You will be pleased to know that we are about to capitalize the city's transportation shortcomings."

The Early Bird's gloom disappeared in the sunshine of a spacious smile, as he realized that the master confidence man had designs upon some improperly chaperoned bank account; that they were about to plunge into the exciting whirl of another of Mr. Clackworthy's delectable adventures.

"Maybe I don't getcha, but th' old bean gets th' notion that you're gonna grab some coin from th' sandbag artists what makes th' long sufferin' public dig down for eight Lincolns for th' priv'lege of havin' their shoes massaged by their fellow passengers. Do I go to th' head of th' class?"

"I regret to say that you have guessed wrong, James. Nothing would, I assure you, give me more undiluted pleasure than to coat my fingers with glue, and dip them into the treasure chest of the so-called street-car barons. Possibly we may at some future time devise ways and means of realizing that laudable ambition, but at present no plan presents itself."

The Early Bird sighed regretfully and again gazed sadly at his mutilated shoes.

"It's cheaper to ride in taxicabs," he mourned. Mr. Clackworthy reproved him with a glance; he liked undivided attention when he was about to outline one of his schemes.

"Speak th' piece, boss; don't you see my ears quiverin'?" apologized The Early Bird.

"James, I do not believe that any one will deny that the city's transportation is wholly inadequate. The surface and elevated lines themselves admit it; the population has grown beyond them. High costs of construction preclude any plans of extension, because the banks refuse to accept present inflated values as a fair basis."

"Shoot lower," pleaded The Early Bird. "You are three syllables beyond my range."

"There has been considerable agitation for a subway," pursued Mr. Clackworthy, "but a 'tube' is expensive even in normal times; and now, with labor and material costs sky-high, no popular-priced fare would permit a subway company to pay the interest on its bonds. The subway plan has been rejected as financially unfeasible."

"You mean th' nickel-grabbers couldn't drag in enough jack t' keep th' subway out of hock?" paraphrased The Early Bird.

"Precisely, James. The popular demand, as you know, is for a five-cent fare. The city administration has been struggling with all sorts of schemes, municipal ownership being most prominently mentioned, to keep the fare within a nickel.

"Several months ago, you may recall, there was considerable publicity given to the proposed monotrack system which is used in some of the European cities."

"I gotcha," agreed The Early Bird. "I seen th' pictures in th' papers. A car hangin' up in th' air on a wire rope — sort of reminded me of th' stunt we used to play when I was a kid in Allen's Alley. We used to give th' cat a ride by slidin' a basket along ma's clothesline."

Mr. Clackworthy chuckled.

"A bit like that, perhaps, James," he admitted. "But to get to the point, the strong feature of the monotrack system was the small cost of construction. The single track would be suspended by the support of an iron framework, the power being supplied by the third-rail system. It would mean much less expense in securing right of way, as much less space would be needed. The heavy roadbed required by the elevated would be unnecessary, and the streets would not be darkened by over-head track structure, simply iron posts at the curbing to sup-port the overhanging rail."

"Why don't they go ahead and build it?" demanded The Early Bird. "With shoes costing eighteen beanos and —"

"The city administration was much in favor of the plan, and even went so far as to grant a franchise to the Monotrack Transit Company," interrupted Mr. Clackworthy. "The com-pany was incorporated for two hundred thousand dollars — just for preliminary organization, you know, and its prospects were so bright that the stock sold for par, and went quite readily, too.

"But you can't float a company on optimism and a fran-chise, James; when the big bankers turned down the scheme, the price of Monotrack tumbled to ten dollars a share and no takers.

"James, I propose that you and I revive poor, dying Mono-track, as it lies at the door of the stock market, gasping its last."

The Early Bird's eyes bulged.

"Great Goshen!" he exclaimed. "You mean your gonna build a car line!"

"How you do jump at conclusions, James. I didn't say that I intended to build a monotrack system — I am merely going to revive the stock."

"I getcha," grinned The Early Bird. "You ain't gonna build it, you're just gonna make some of these rich birds think you're gonna build it."

"Yes, that's what I propose to have them think — about one hundred thousand dollars worth," said Mr. Clackworthy.

II.

Mrs. Clara Cartwright was a sweet but not nearly so trusting a woman as she had been six months before. The reason for her recently developed skepticism regarding the sincerity of mankind reposed carelessly in a bureau drawer of her modest home. Four highly engraved and very prosperous looking stock certificates showed her to be the possessor of two thousand shares of stock in the Monotrack Transit Company.

She had come into possession of this stock upon the payment of sixty thousand dollars in cash, which was every cent that her deeply lamented husband had left her through the medium of a life insurance policy, to smooth the rocky road of otherwise impoverished widowhood. She had purchased the stock upon the advice of Cyrus Prindivale, president of the Suburban Trust Company, who had been her husband's banker and who, naturally enough, became her trusted business adviser.

Cyrus Prindivale was a moneymaker, attesting to the soundness of his business judgment; but, the vital point which Mrs. Cartwright overlooked was that Mr. Prindivale was quite in the habit of counting his gain, while some one else was tabulating corresponding loss. The suburban banker, to be extremely charitable, was not governed by any exalted rules of ethics, and, except for the rich cloak of respectability that he had wrapped about him, one might have been tempted to charge, in the plainest of words, that he was a crook. Other bankers and business men were accustomed to scrutinize carefully the commas, semicolons, and periods of all papers and documents which involved them in any sort of transaction with Mr. Prindivale.

The financial genius of the somewhat fashionable suburb had been one of the prime movers in the organization of the Monotrack Transit Company. As new corporations are allowed twenty percent of their capital for the floating of their stock and organization purposes, Mr. Prindivale had purchased two thousand shares at a generous discount. It had, in fact, cost him only twenty dollars per share, while others not in on the ground floor, were forced to write their checks for its par value of a hundred dollars.

For a time Mr. Prindivale shared the optimism of the scheme's other promoters, that Monotrack was going to be a bonanza, but his shrewd little gimletlike eyes, accustomed to looking considerable distances into the future, soon saw the handwriting of the city's big financiers across the resplendent, gilt-sealed Monotrack certificates, and he read: "Nothing doing."

At almost precisely the same moment he recalled the sixty thousand dollar balance on the books of his bank, to the credit of Mrs. Clara Cartwright, the full amount of her check from the life insurance company. The very same day Mrs. Cartwright, in her widow's weeds, happened into the bank, and Mr. Prindivale, in his soft, suave voice, painted a glowing and enticing picture of the wealth that was to be made out of Monotrack Transit. So cleverly did he bait his gold hook that Mrs. Cartwright was pleading with him to be allowed to invest.

And, "only because your husband was such a dear friend of mine, Mrs. Cartwright," Mr. Prindivale permitted the widow to write him a check for sixty thousand dollars. The price was fixed by a simple process of multiplication; two thousand shares at thirty dollars per share equals sixty thousand dollars — and sixty thousand dollars was all she had.

So Cyrus Prindivale was in actual cash some twenty thousand dollars richer as a result of his almost disastrous dream concerning the success of Monotrack Transit. But there was one thing which Mr. Prindivale did not know; Mrs. Clara Cartwright was a first cousin of Mr. Amos Clackworthy.

III.

On the nineteenth floor of the Great Lakes Building was a most elegantly furnished office suite of two rooms. The lettering on the corridor door informed one that it was occupied by the "Atlas Investment Company." In the outer room a very pretty young woman was seated before a mahogany typewriter desk; she was reading a popular novel, but the drawer of the desk was conveniently open, ready to conceal this evidence of her lack of occupation; there was also a sheet of paper in the machine, for instant use. The fetching typist was none other than Mrs. George Bascom, wife of one of Mr. Amos Clackworthy's lieutenants.

A draftsman's board stood conspicuously in one corner; it held some half completed drawings, bearing the words, "Monotrack Transit Company." Seated in front of the draftsman's board was George Bascom, who, at the present moment, was using the point of his dividers to clean his ring, which, in truth, was about the only use he could make of them.

Within the inner room, the door of which was marked "private," a tall, businesslike man with a superbly trimmed Vandyke beard was seated at his massive mahogany desk; it was, of course, Mr. Clackworthy.

The Early Bird, who had deserted his own desk in the outer office, was seated in the private office, and his eyes roved admiringly about.

"Some joint!" he ejaculated. "Yeah, I'll say it's some joint."

"James," remonstrated Mr. Clackworthy, "your idiomatic English is most refreshing — on occasions; but it becomes my duty to remind you that you are now the private secretary of a most conservative investment broker, and, as such, you must speak with more refinement."

"Don't worry th' old think-box into a headache," retorted The Early Bird. "I'll can th' lowbrow chatter when th' lamb appears for shearin'. Huh! I'll twist th' old tongue around so's this bird'll lamp me and say: 'Ha-vard, eh?'"

Mr. Clackworthy selected a fresh cigar.

"James," he mused, "human nature is very contradictory. How often do we reject the truth and yet receive falsehood with childish credulity."

"Th' bottomless pit's only knee-deep compared with your lingo," mourned The Early Bird, not without admiration for Mr. Clackworthy's rhetorical facility.

"Here is an example of my philosophy," continued Mr. Clackworthy. "If I went to the Blackmere Hotel with seventeen trunks and a valet, and announced that I was a millionaire, no one would believe me; yet if I went to the same hotel with the same trappings and denied that I was a millionaire, every one would be quite convinced that I was.

"Well, James, that is the philosophy upon which our present little venture is founded. I do not think that it can fail."

IV.

Mr. Cyrus Prindivale tilted back in his swivel-chair, and

his heavy eyebrows over his beady little eyes contracted into a puzzled frown. Five separate and distinct times he digested the contents of the letter. Carefully he crinkled the edge of the heavy vellum parchment between his critical fingers, and caressed the unimpeachably engraved letters which announced "Atlas Investment Company, 1924-26, Great Lakes Building." The letterhead was dignified, bespeaking taste and refinement.

"Never heard of 'em," muttered Mr. Prindivale. "It may amount to something, though." The letter read:

> We are given to understand that you are the owner of two thousand shares of stock in the Monotrack Transit Company. We are delegated by a client of ours to purchase a controlling amount of this stock in order that he may acquire the plans and specifications which belong to the company. We are empowered to offer you the present market price of ten dollars per share. As you are well aware, the revival of the company is a financial impossibility, and our client has no other reason for acquiring this stock than to become the owner in fee simple of its drawings, which, he hopes, may be an asset at some future time.

"Humph!" grunted Mr. Prindivale. "They're too darn emphatic about wanting 'only the plans and specifications.' There is, I suspect, a fox in the henhouse; this is well worth looking into."

Being, himself, a man of devious methods it was natural that he should look with cautious suspicion on the all too positive frankness of others. With a frown he remembered that he was no longer the possessor of two thousand shares of Monotrack Transit, but, remembering the frantic expostulations of Mrs. Clara Cartwright upon her discovery that her sixty thousand dollars' worth of elaborate certificates was utterly worthless, he anticipated no difficulty in buying it back for, say, ten dollars a share.

Mr. Prindivale pressed the button on his desk and summoned Dawes, the cashier, who was widely acquainted with many details of the city's financial circle.

"Dawes," said Mr. Prindivale, "just who are the Atlas Investment Company?"

Running his fingers through his thin hair, Dawes turned to the "A" compartment of his card-indexed mind, but shook his head.

"Name vaguely familiar, Mr. Prindivale, but I don't seem to place them," he replied regretfully. "However, I will find out."

Dawes stepped to the telephone and called one of the downtown financial houses; a moment later he returned.

"Fisher & Fisher have just told me, Mr. Prindivale, that the Atlas people are an — an — exclusively small concern, soliciting no public business of any character; it is well understood that they are the private agents for a very reputable financier and that, in short, they confine their activities to handling the confidential matters of" — Mr. Dawes paused impressively — "of J. K."

Mr. Prindivale started violently.

"Merciful Heaven!" he gasped. "J. K.!"

J. K., it must be explained, was a name to conjure with among financial circles; J. K. were the well-known initials of Mr. James K. Easterday, president of three big banks and financial power extraordinary. What he said was financial law.

It was not, to be sure, within Mr. Prindivale's province to know, that the original Atlas Investment Company had, a few days before, removed their offices from the Great Lakes Building, and that Mr. Clackworthy had hurriedly leased them, neglecting to remove the neat gilt lettering from the door.

V.

As Mr. Prindivale opened the door of 1924 Great Lakes Building, the scene of luxuriant solidity was, somehow, just as he had pictured it. Mrs. George Bascom, her novel hurriedly consigned to the desk drawer as the caller's shadow fell across the door's glass panel, hurried her slim fingers over the typewriter keyboard.

Over in the corner George Bascom wrinkled his brow studiously over his draftsman's board.

"I wish to see Mr. Clackworthy," announced Mr. Prindivale.

"Busy just at this moment," politely responded the pretty

stenographer and nodded to a chair. The chair, it happened, through careful calculation, was within easy vision of the drafting board. As Mr. Prindivale strained his neck forward for a closer inspection of the drawings, Mr. Bascom glanced at him suspiciously and rudely draped a large piece of paper over the mass of lines and angles, but not before Mr. Prindivale's sharp little eyes had seen the words "Monotrack Transit Company."

"Ah!" breathed Mr. Prindivale. "Secrecy! I knew that something was on foot. Foxy old J. K."

Inside the private office Mr. Clackworthy calmly smoked his cigar, and marked time until the suburban banker should have waited a sufficient length of time. The master confidence man had adopted none of his long list of pseudonyms in this adventure, for he had carefully laid his plans strictly within legal bounds. Even his possession of the abandoned offices of the Atlas Investment Company and the use of that name on his letterheads were entirely according to law. With customary thoroughness for detail he had discovered that the genuine concern had neglected the little formality of registering with the secretary of state, thus leaving it open to use by others; and Mr. Clackworthy had spent the required incorporation fee of appropriating it, free of possible future embarrassing entanglements.

A moment later The Early Bird, hurrying in from the street with an armful of important-looking documents, paused at Mrs. Bascom's desk. He sighed and mopped his brow.

"Say," whispered Mrs. Bascom, making sure that it was loud enough to be heard across the room, "you'd better hurry up with those papers; Mr. Clackworthy's in a big hurry for them — J. K. is in there with him and they want them quick."

Hastily James Early grabbed up the documents and hurried into the inside office. Eagerly Mr. Prindivale leaned forward to catch a stray word or sentence that might filter through the heavy door, but, to his chagrin, it was sound proof.

"Well, Old Gimlet Eye's out there waitin'," he announced.

"Yes, I know." said Mr. Clackworthy; "Mrs. Bascom pressed the buzzer a moment ago. How do you size him up?"

"As nervous as a Pennsylvania millionaire about to meet King George," chuckled The Early Bird; "say, that guy —"

"Watch your English, James."

"Well, as I was gonna say, if you keep that gink — that man, I mean — out there very long he's gonna wear th' seat out of his pants th' way he's squirming around in th' chair."

"That's fine, James; now you may retire to the outer office while I complete my conference with — ah — J. K. Remember my instructions and follow them to the letter."

The Early Bird bowed solemnly to the empty chair across from Mr. Clackworthy, grinned, and made for the door.

"I've got it down pat," he said.

In the outer office, James went to his desk, which stood but a few feet from where Mr. Prindivale was seated. Slowly he began to sort over a stack of papers which were heaped in front of him.

Mr. Prindivale edged his chair a few inches closer.

"Have a cigar," he invited; "fine tobacco, very fine; import 'em myself direct. You have a very nice office here."

"Uh-huh," muttered The Early Bird, ignoring the cigar.

"By the way," probed Mr. Prindivale, "I thought I saw my old friend J. K. — fellow banker of mine, you know — come in just ahead of me, does he transact much business with this firm?"

The Early Bird frowned in apparent annoyance.

"Never heard of 'im," he mumbled, impolitely taking a cigar from his own pocket and lighting it, but, at the same time, he averted his eyes.

"Never heard of J. K.?" scoffed Mr. Prindivale with entirely justified skepticism. "Ha! Ha! That is quite a joke — sort of in the class with the fellow down in Arkansas who, when the orator shouted: 'Lincoln is dead,' declared that he didn't even know that Lincoln was sick."

"Never heard of 'im," repeated The Early Bird with ridiculous obstinacy.

"I see," nodded Mr. Prindivale, "it's a dark secret; oh, I'm on."

"On to what?"

"I know J. K. mighty well — personal friend of mine."

"Uh-huh," grunted The Early Bird noncommittally, and

his pencil beat a little tattoo on his desk. In accordance with this signal, George Bascom removed the improvised paper shield from the draftsman's board.

"Bascom!" snapped James. "I don't want any more work on that just now; hasn't Mr. Clackworthy told you —"

Hastily Bascom restored the pushpins and Mr. Prindivale's nostrils quivered.

"Something big on foot — something mighty big," he thought, and he leaned back in his chair, contracted his eyes thoughtfully and sought to reason it out.

VI.

At the end of thirty minutes Mr. Clackworthy gave the button on his desk three swift jabs and The Early Bird appeared.

"I got 'im goin'," chuckled James. "He tried to pump me for all he was worth about this J. K. stuff."

"James, you chew tobacco on occasions, do you not?" queried Mr. Clackworthy.

"Chew!" repeated The Early Bird. "Now, ain't that a question to ask a guy — with th' little lamb outside waitin' for th' clippers. Gonna get me to sign th' pledge?"

Mr. Clackworthy took from his desk a fresh plug of natural twist.

"James," he chuckled, "you know that I abhor the vile habit, even in others; can't touch it myself; but it now becomes necessary for me to ask you to masticate a generous portion of this plug of tobacco. Strew it around somewhere in the general vicinity of that seventy-five dollar cuspidor. No, I'm not jesting; it's part of the stage setting."

Quietly The Early Bird complied.

"That's all, James," said Mr. Clackworthy; "I will see Mr. Prindivale now."

"Holy blue-eyed catfish!" muttered The Early Bird as he retired.

A moment later Mr. Prindivale entered, glancing swiftly about. The first thing that caught his eye was the dark tobacco stains which decorated the floor; he smiled in triumph.

"Ah!" he exclaimed. "Looks as if my old friend J. K. had

been here." J. K. Easterday's careless way of chewing tobacco was notorious in moneyed circles.

"J. K. Who?" demanded Mr. Clackworthy.

"As if there were more than one J. K. Easterday," said Mr. Prindivale, exceedingly pleased with himself at this masterful bit of deduction.

"J. K. Easterday has not been here," declared Mr. Clackworthy with entirely truthful but perhaps unnecessary emphasis. "What would that big fellow be doing up here in my humble domain? You honor me."

"Have it your way," said Mr. Prindivale, plainly unconvinced.

"Mr. Prindivale," began Mr. Clackworthy briskly, "I know that you are a busy man and I will not take your time by lengthy and needless explanations. My letter frankly explained the matter. You have two thousand shares of Monotrack Transit that you couldn't sell for a scrap of paper. The last selling price was ten dollars a share. For the purpose stated in my letter to you, my client is willing to give you the last quoted market price. That's the whole thing in a nutshell. Did you bring the shares with you?"

"Tut! Tut!" remonstrated Mr. Prindivale craftily. "Not so fast; I'm too old a head to be rushed like that. Come, my dear sir; give me credit for a little intelligence. When I play stud poker I like to see a few of the cards on the table before I bet."

"You are intimating —"

"Intimating nothing, Mr. Clackworthy; I know for a positive fact that you've got an ace up your sleeve."

"I have stated the proposition just as it —"

"Just as it isn't," charged Mr. Prindivale belligerently. "I've got two thousand shares of Monotrack Transit; some one wants them — that somebody happens to be J. K. — and when old J.K. wants anything he pays the price for it — if he has to."

"You are entirely misleading yourself, Mr. Prindivale," declared Mr. Clackworthy with a frankness which the suburban banker little suspected. "J. K. Easterday has nothing to do with this matter."

"Hasn't, eh?" cried Mr. Prindivale exultantly, pointing his finger at a mass of papers which littered the big mahogany conference table. "Then maybe you can explain that."

He gestured toward the exposed edge of one of the closely typewritten pages; there, penned in scrawling but entirely legible characters, were the somewhat cryptic letters:

"OKEH JK."

"Don't tell me!" he shouted, now thoroughly excited by the importance of his discovery. "That's J. K. Easterday's O. K. mark — Okeh, the Indian mark of approval; there are only two men in America who write it that way, one is the President of the United States and the other is J. K. Easterday."

"Bosh!" retorted Mr. Clackworthy; but, nevertheless, showing considerable chagrin. "I wrote that down there myself — you are jumping at conclusions." Mr. Clackworthy was showing a most remarkable tenacity for the strict letter of truth.

"Lay the cards down on the table and I'll talk turkey," bantered Mr. Prindivale.

"Really, Mr. Prindivale, you are getting rather needlessly excited; I wish to play a game of golf this afternoon and I want to get this business over with. Suppose we say fifteen dollars a share."

"It cost me more than that; I made up my mind that I'd hold onto that stock until I came out whole on it or let the paper rot."

"Well, Mr. Prindivale, if you really feel that way about it, possibly we could pay you a price that would permit you to recover your original investment; you did not, I am reliably informed, pay the par value."

"Ha!" exulted Mr. Prindivale. "I trapped you that time; so it's worth something after all, eh? How much is it worth? Come across; remember you are not dealing with a grammar-school student, but a business man."

Mr. Clackworthy stroked his Vandyke beard meditatively; at the same time his foot slid under the desk and touched the tip of the electric button which was secreted there. It connected with a faint-voiced alarm on The Early Bird's desk, and James Early, in turn, touched a button which connected directly with the telephone on Mr. Clackworthy's desk. The bell tinkled.

In the act of lifting the receiver from the book, Mr. Clackworthy turned to the suburban banker.

"Granting, for the sake of reaching an agreement, that you paid the par value of one hundred dollars a share and, taking cognizance of your determination to come out whole on it, I am empowered to offer you —"

The bell rang insistently.

"Hello," said Mr. Clackworthy into the transmitter. "Yes, this is Mr. Clackworthy; yes, Aubuchon — uh-huh — yes, I understand. He's here now."

Mr. Prindivale, sensing a personal reference, looked up quickly; he saw that Mr. Clackworthy's gaze had grown hard and cold; the air of eagerness as he had jockeyed for the best possible price was gone. The banker, with a sinking heart, realized that something had gone wrong.

"Mr. Prindivale," said Mr. Clackworthy curtly, hanging up the receiver, "there is no need to discuss this matter further. I find that I shall not need to buy the stock from you, after all."

"But — but — I don't understand," stammered Mr. Prindivale.

"Oh, yes, I think you do," returned Mr. Clackworthy icily. "One of my men has reported to me just now that you sold your Monotrack holdings some months ago — to some woman; we shall, of course, deal directly with the holder of the stock. You almost hooked me, eh?"

Mr. Prindivale grabbed his hat and fled.

VII.

There was a reason for Mr. Prindivale's precipitate departure. He cursed because the elevators were so slow and bolted out of the entrance to the drug store at the corner where he knew there was a telephone pay station.

His fingers, fumbling with eager haste, turned the leaves of the directory until he found the name of Mrs. Clara Cartwright. It was, of course, a suburban call and he muttered trenchant maledictions for the operator who seemed to deliberately delay his connection. After five anguished and perspiring minutes Mrs. Cartwright's soft voice identified itself from the other end of the wire.

"Mrs. Cartwright," gulped Mr. Prindivale, striving to make his tone normal, "about the Monotrack stock which I sold you — er — I have been thinking it over and I realize that it was — er — entirely upon your faith in my advice that you purchased it. I — I could not, in all — er — fairness, expect you to pay for the burden of my — ah — sincere but mistaken judgment, so I have decided to take the stock off your hands without a cent of loss to you and pocket it myself."

"Oh, Mr. Prindivale! How lovely of you!" exclaimed Mrs. Cartwright, who had been carefully tutored by her cousin's husband, Mr. Clackworthy, for this identical situation.

"Yes," went on Mr. Prindivale, "so I will be right out and give you a check."

"Oh, there is no hurry, Mr. Prindivale, so long as you promise."

"But there is a hur — I mean that I am in a hurry to get it off my mind. I know you will feel better with things fixed up; I — Well, I might die tonight, you know. There has been no one out to see you about buying the stock, I suppose?"

"Oh, no; who would want to buy it?"

"Oh, of course not; of course not," assented the banker, "but — um — in case some one did talk to you about it, I would advise you to do nothing until you talk to me."

"Oh, Mr. Prindivale!" gurgled Mrs. Cartwright. "You are so excited and everything; I do believe that the stock is going up."

The banker swore under his breath; he was walking on dangerously thin ice.

"Certainly not; that was just — just a little joke," he amended.

A taxicab driver, bribed with a twenty-dollar bill, broke all the speed records in getting Mr. Prindivale out to the suburb. The banker found Mrs. Cartwright in the sitting room of her modest little home, evidently waiting for him; she had the stock certificates in her hand.

"I'll just write a check, Mrs. Cartwright," he said with hardly the ceremony of a greeting.

"Why, Mr. Prindivale!" the widow exclaimed. "You act so excited. I do believe that something has happened to the

Monotrack business."

Mentally the banker reviled woman for her intuitive powers, as he wrote his check.

"Here you are," he said, unable to keep the eagerness from his voice; "I will take the stock back now — you see I have not allowed you to lose a cent."

Mrs. Cartwright tilted her chin and firmly put her hand which held the certificates behind her back.

"I've got — what do you men call it — a hunch?" she said. "I have decided not to sell for thirty dollars a share!"

Mr. Prindivale tried a bluff; with an anger which was not entirely assumed, he snapped his check book shut and pocketed his pen.

"Just as you will," he said coldly; "I try to play good Samaritan and am at once suspected of some underhand scheme to cheat you."

"I — I am sorry if I have misjudged you," she returned with a show of penitence. "Of course, if you are sincere in your offer, I suppose —" She paused in sudden thought. "But I can't get rid of that — that hunch; something seems to tell that I should not sell my stock for thirty dollars a share."

"And I presume," said Mr. Prindivale with a poorly concealed sarcasm, "that your hunch also tells you just what price you will get."

"Now, let's see!" she cried, like a child playing a game and clapping her hands in fun. "Now, isn't that funny — a figure just pops in my mind — eighty dollars a share!"

"Come, Mrs. Cartwright," purred Mr. Prindivale in his most persuasive tone, "I'll tell you what I will do. Since I have caused you quite a little worry over your apparent loss of sixty thousand dollars, I will permit you to make a little profit — out of my own pocket, you know — as a sort of penalty for my mistaken judgment in advising you. I will give you thirty-five dollars a share."

Mrs. Cartwright laughed, and how was Mr. Prindivale to know that this was the cue for Mrs. Cartwright's loyal and trusted servant, Amelia, to connect the electric current which caused a telephone bell to ring in another room? The banker was engulfed by apprehension, that might be J. K.'s men seeking to get in touch with her; he was, somehow, almost sure that it was.

"As — as I was saying" — he stumbled.

"Mis' Cartwright; there's a man on the phone as wants to talk to you," said Amelia; "he says his name's Clack — Clack something."

"Just a minute, Mr. Prindivale; you will excuse me for a moment."

"Wait! Wait!" cried Mr. Prindivale wildly. "Let us close this up before you go; now let me see —" He was hastily doing a little problem in mental arithmetic; Clackworthy had promised to pay the par value of one hundred dollars per share, that would be an even two hundred thousand dollars. If he paid Mrs. Cartwright eighty dollars a share that would total one hundred and sixty thousand dollars, and as hard as the bargain was, a forty-thousand-dollar profit as compared with the clean-up of a cool one hundred and forty thousand dollars that he had visioned was, after all, a good killing.

"You said that you would take eighty dollars a share," pursued the banker.

"Oh, but I was just joking — really; surely you —"

"You gave me your word, your promise, that you would take eighty dollars a share," insisted Mr. Prindivale. "You can't back out now; you must let me have it — you must!"

Feverishly he again wrote in his check book; he forced the slip of paper into Mrs. Cartwright's fingers and almost forcibly tore the stock certificates from her hand. The widow was apparently too bewildered to protest. And before she could find voice, Mr. Prindivale dashed out of the house. He would have been a much surprised and mystified man if he could have seen her rush to the telephone and call a city number and to have heard her words:

"Amos Clackworthy, you darling, darling man! We have met the enemy and his check is ours. I'm going to rush right out, just like you told me, and have it certified — then I will be right down and give you your hundred thousand dollar collection fee. Isn't it great to have a cousin who has a husband with such a wonderful brain!"

VIII.

And that would end the story, except for Mr. Prindivale being what is sometimes sneeringly referred to as "a rotten loser."

When the suburban banker trotted triumphantly up to the Great Lakes Building the following day, two thousand shares of Monotrack Transit in his pocket, he was amazed to find the offices of the Atlas Investment Company vacant. It gradually dawned upon him that something was wrong. In his first burst of rage he visited the district attorney's office and laid bare the amazing story.

The district attorney, viewing the case from all angles, decided that perhaps morally Mr. Cyrus Prindivale had been most thoroughly bunkoed, but that legally he had merely made an unfortunate investment. The district attorney, too, in delving deep into the details, had uncovered the fact that the worthless stock Mr. Prindivale had purchased from Mrs. Cartwright for one hundred and sixty thousand dollars was the same identical and equally worthless stock that he had sold to her for just one hundred thousand dollars less than that amount. And the prosecutor bowed Mr. Prindivale out of the office with scant sympathy.

By rare coincidence, the district attorney was a nephew of no less illustrious person than J. K. Easterday, and that was how "J. K." got hold of it and may explain an otherwise mysterious communication which Mr. Amos Clackworthy received in his morning mail.

Mr. Clackworthy and The Early Bird were at breakfast when the Japanese boy entered with the postman's nine o'clock delivery. From under the edge of the white tablecloth protruded the glossy surface of one of The Early Bird's new twenty-dollar shoes; he glanced at the shining patent leather and grinned.

"Twenty smackers this time — and worth it," he said. "You gotta pay real dough for kicks these days, and this pair ain't gonna get chawed up by no plebeian — that's right, ain't it — sodbusters. That Monotrack layout sure has improved th' transportation situation for yours truly, James; I went down on Boul Mich yesterday, and laid out two thousand iron men for th' niftiest little racer that ever landed a guy in th' speeders' court."

Mr. Clackworthy, laughing silently, as he read the contents of one of the envelopes which he had just opened, tossed it over to The Early Bird.

"Speaking, James, of our most recent adventure," he said, "you will, I think, find this the crowning touch."

The Early Bird picked up the sheet of paper; there was but one typewritten sentence which said:

It is gossiped in financial circles that Cyrus Prindivale, an exceedingly shrewd banker, has recently endowed the School of Experience with the munificent gift of one hundred thousand dollars.

Scrawled across one corner in a bold, masterful hand were the letters: "Okeh J. K."

MR. CLACKWORTHY WITHIN THE LAW

AS a dinner host Mr. Amos Clackworthy was faultless. He knew how to order a meal, how to smuggle in now forbidden appetizers, and how to keep his guests in a sparkling good humor. He sat at the head of a table in a secluded corner of the exclusive Blackmere Hotel's dining room, where the cuisine and the prices are things to make one gasp. At his right, proudly convex of chest in his new one-hundred-and-fifty dollar evening clothes, sat James Early, trying with commendable diligence to remember his forks and forget his slang. Although Mr. Clackworthy enjoyed The Early Bird's quaint idioms on most occasions, James knew that the Blackmere was a place where one must be on one's dignity.

The other two members of Mr. Clackworthy's party were George Bascom and George's pretty, clever, and vivacious little wife, both of whom very frequently assisted the master confidence man in his pleasantly profitable but somewhat unethical profession.

The Early Bird was in a gay mood, for he was entertaining the eager hope that Mr. Clackworthy, strategist par excellence in his own private little warfare on bloated bank balances, would serve them, in lieu of sparkling burgundy, wine of excitement in the shape of one of the new plans which his fertile brain was always developing. As the dinner progressed, and there was still no hint of the expected scheme, James began to get fidgety; his high collar began to saw his neck, and he splashed his coffee. Impulsively he released the brakes, so to speak, on his pent-up vocabulary.

"Say," he mumbled plaintively, "ain'tcha ever gonna play the record? Didn'tcha come here t' do nothin' besides eat?"

Mr. Clackworthy frowned severely; he had especially warned The Early Bird to be on his best behavior. James subsided with a leaden heart, for there was missing from the master confidence man's eye that sly twinkle which so often bespoke a teasing inclination to keep him guessing.

And then came the second cloud to mar the success of the dinner. Mrs. Bascom, glancing through the screen of palms which surrounded their table, suddenly ceased to smile. Her soft blue eyes showed a hint of angry fire.

"Caleb Denton!" she murmured, her slim fingers clutching viciously about her salad fork; one would have guessed that she was wishing it was this man's neck rather than the unoffending salad fork which felt the wicked pressure. "I had forgotten he existed, the — the old thief!"

Mr. Clackworthy, distressed that anything should mar a guest's enjoyment of a perfect meal perfectly served, leaned forward.

"Don't think about anything unpleasant, please," he urged. "The sight of some diner, I take it, has revived unpleasant memories. Let the past bury its dead, the sages have told us."

"But that old Caleb Denton isn't buried!" she replied. "I suppose he is one of those people who are too mean to die. Oh, dear me! Why did he have to dine here tonight? He hasn't entered my mind for years."

"I have always found," said Mr. Clackworthy, "that when one has something on one's mind the best way to dispose of the mental burden is to share it with some one else. Just who is this Caleb Denton, and what particular piece of iniquity has he been guilty of?"

"It's a long story," said Mrs. Bascom, sighing, "but perhaps I can synopsize it, and —"

Her sentence was interrupted by a tiny gasp as a sudden inspiration took possession of her thoughts. "And," she went on with a hopeful emphasis, "maybe, Mr. Clackworthy, you could — could help me even up the score with Caleb Denton! Oh, I wonder if you could? The old skinflint!"

The Early Bird, who until this moment felt only a bored indifference in Mrs. Bascom's prospective tale of a past injustice, leaned forward with a suddenness which landed his cuff in the butter.

"Why, sure!" he exclaimed. "Speak the piece, missus, an' the boss'll sharpen up the old harpoon for this here bozo. Won't you, boss?"

"Naturally," said Mr. Clackworthy, smiling with modest

caution, "I should be most happy to assist George and his wife to even up a score, but it would be rather impulsive to make an unqualified promise without more data."

"It isn't my score," murmured George, frowning a little as if peeved to discover that his wife had a secret from him. "I never heard of this Caleb Denton. Who is he, Nada? And" — his voice took on a belligerently rising inflection — "what did that bald-headed old turtle ever do to you?"

Mrs. Bascom gave her husband's hand a reassuring pat and thanked him for his show of loyalty with a smile.

"Don't worry, Georgie," she replied. "He never tried to kidnap me, and what he did was to the family, rather than to me personally — although it did affect me personally. Besides, if it hadn't been for 'that bald-headed old turtle' the chances are that I would have never come to Chicago, and you would never have met me."

"Then I forgive him, even be his sins as black as Satan's," said George with fervor. "How come I never heard of him?"

"I had really forgotten him until tonight," said Mrs. Bascom. "He's from my home town; I haven't seen him since I left there, and he was responsible for my leaving. Dear! Dear! Those were the sad days!"

The Early Bird stared appraisingly at the solitary diner on the other side of the palms, whom Mrs. Bascom had pointed out as Caleb Denton. Under Mr. Clackworthy's tutelage James prided himself that he had absorbed considerable proficiency in the complex art of reading human nature. He saw a thin, slump-shouldered, wizen-faced man of perhaps sixty-odd, with quick, cunning eyes. His hairless head was onion-shiny. The stamp of rural life was upon him but failed to disguise a calculating shrewdness. It was easy to picture his long, bent fingers in the miser's clutch.

"Huh!" grunted The Early Bird. "I got that goof's number aw'right. He's gotta case on the lady what whispers word of love from the front side of the good old American dollar. Every mornin' when he starts in on the day's business he moistens his fingers with glue t' keep any Lincolns from slippin' away from him. Separatin' that perumbulatin' billiard ball from the coin of the realm is just as easy as — well, walkin' untouched through burning oil. Mrs. Bascom here ain't let us in on the know, but I'm layin' a century note against the price of an L ticket that he pried her folks loose from a bundle of jack."

Mrs. Bascom nodded vigorously.

"Let her proceed with her story," suggested Mr. Clackworthy.

"I can tell it very briefly," began Mrs. Bascom. "I spent my childhood in Liptonville, Illinois. My father owned a hardware store and only made a fair living. He invented a new kind of plow and had to borrow money at Caleb Denton's bank — Mr. Denton owns the bank, you know — to go ahead with the experiments. Denton loaned him all the money he wanted, several thousand dollars, on 'demand' notes. The notes were secured by mortgages on dad's store and our home. Then, just before the plow was ready to realize on, Denton suddenly swooped down like the old vulture that he is and demanded payment. Of course dad couldn't pay, and Denton took the store, our little home and — worse still — all the patents; they had been put up for security, too. I'm afraid that my father wasn't a very shrewd business man — and Denton was.

"Dad was frozen out. Denton took the patents and sold them to one of the big harvester companies for twenty-five thousand dollars. Dad died soon after, from the disappointment, we always thought — and mother was left alone in the world with three little kiddies. I was the oldest. There wasn't any way to make a living in Liptonville and — and that's why we came to Chicago. That's the story."

George Bascom's hands clenched as, in his imagination, he got a strangle hold on Caleb Denton's protruding Adam's apple. The Early Bird smiled, but not from amusement; he was merely pleased that his judgment concerning Mr. Denton had been correct.

Mr. Clackworthy's eyelids lowered meditatively as he stared through the palms upon the cold, hard face of the Liptonville banker.

"Mrs. Bascom," he said gravely, "the firm of Clackworthy and Company accepts the task of collecting an old account for you — with all of the interest possible. And, you may be assured, you shall have the pleasure of taking a most active part in it."

The Early Bird remembered where he was just in time to

check a whoop that would have caused various and sundry Indians, peacefully bleaching their bones since what is now Chicago was Fort Dearborn and a remote pioneer settlement in the then kingdom of the redskin, to turn over in their graves with envy.

"I knowed it!" he said exultantly. "I knowed we was gonna have something b'sides food at this here blowout. Cheat the cheater, that's my motter. Boss don't leave that guy so much as a lid t' pertect that fly's skatin'-rink of his from the Lake Michigan breezes!"

II.

Liptonville was just an average sort of town with an average lot of people. The Commercial Club had boasted of three thousand population until the census takers came along and established the fact that an actual count of noses made the correct figure two thousand seven hundred and twenty-nine.

Like all small towns Liptonville has its "big man." And that big man, measuring largeness by purely monetary standards as we humans are so apt to do, was Caleb Denton, president of the Liptonville State Bank, president of the Liptonville Broom Factory, largest stockholder in the Liptonville Stores Company, with his greedy old fingers in almost every one of the other local financial pies.

If Liptonville had not been so awed by Denton's opulence and Midaslike touch its people might have hated him; perhaps a great many of them did, but if such was the case they took particular pains to keep their mouths shut. By dint of domineering ruthlessness in his business methods, feeble attempts to start a rival bank had failed, with the result that at some time or another almost every one in Liptonville had to go to Caleb Denton for money. And he had a most annoying way of refusing to lend money to those who crossed him.

With not a soul in the world to benefit by his mounting fortune, with not a single charitable inclination or impulse, one might have thought that Caleb Denton would grow weary of his continual dollar squeezing and penny shaving, but not so; money mania is as unreasoning as any other mania.

On a Thursday afternoon in September the 4:15 from Chicago disgorged, among other passengers, a slim, most attractive young woman who wore a fashionably tailored suit of gray tricotine. You have guessed it; she was Mrs. George Bascom, and she was alone.

At the Globe Hotel, just across the street from the depot — they still call the railroad station "depot" in Liptonville — she registered, giving as she did so a searching glance at the man behind the desk, who carried himself with that authority which at once labeled him as the proprietor. She knew by the V-shaped scar across his cheek that he was Bud Loomis.

"Why, Bud Loomis!" she cried in genuine pleasure, for Bud was one of several who, in the pinafore days, had fought for the right to carry her books home from school. "Don't you remember me — Nada Ramsey?"

"Gosh!" and Bud gulped. "So it is." As he took her hand he made no attempt to mask his open admiration. "Back on a visit, are you, Nada?"

"I'm not quite sure, Bud," Mrs. Bascom said, laughing. "I got hungry for the home town and just came back. Maybe I'll stay. It's really home to me. The old house — dad's house, you know — is it — is it —"

"Still here, Nada," he replied, "and a good deal like it always was, except they've put in a bathroom, an' a furnace, an' a sun-parlor, an' a sleepin' porch, an' a few little things like that. Solly Henderson's got it now, but his wife died last month, an' he's movin' to the city."

Mrs. Bascom gave a little gasp of sincere delight. Here was a kind stroke of fortune.

"Oh!" she cried. "I wonder — I wonder if he would rent it — furnished? Do you think he would?"

"I dunno," replied Bud. "But you can ask him if you wanna. He lives here at the hotel; there he comes in the door now."

And the result was that Mrs. Bascom found things moving more swiftly than she had anticipated. Within little more than an hour after her return to Liptonville she had rented her old home — not really the same, of course, with all its modernized alterations — and had, as well, taken an option for its purchase at a price of $4,500 provided that she really decided to make her home in Liptonville.

The following day she took complete possession, moving in her three trunks. That same afternoon she paid a visit to the Liptonville State Bank.

As she entered old Caleb Denton was sitting at his desk behind the mahogany railing to one side of the tellers' and cashier's cages.

"Mr. Denton, isn't it?" Mrs. Bascom said sweetly as she paused at the railing. "So glad to see you after all these years, Mr. Denton. Of course you don't remember me — Nada Ramsey?"

Denton's tight-drawn, parchmentlike skin drew up at the corners of his mouth into what he doubtless considered his very best smile, and his bent fingers extended in a mechanically hospitable handshake. He had no feeling of embarrassment toward the daughter of the man whom he had robbed of a comparative fortune; it was only one of many somewhat similar transactions. Had he thought of it at all it would have been only a hazy incident in his mind.

"Yes?" he queried.

"I am thinking of coming back to Liptonville to live," she told him. "Don't you think it's a nice sentiment — coming back to your childhood town?"

"Yes, quite so; quite so," agreed Denton in his sharp, rasping voice. "I understand." Which, of course, he didn't; having no sentiment himself, he could not understand it in some one else.

"I am arranging to buy my old home — dad's old home," she went on. "I have taken an option on it."

Caleb Denton's eyebrows lifted ever so slightly. If she was going to buy property that meant one thing — she had money. He was always more or less interested in persons who had money. At that he was surprised that the daughter of Louis Ramsey, trusting, free-handed, unbusinesslike, should have money. Such a thing wasn't in the blood.

"And I'm going to have the best times," she gushed on. "I am going to have my car brought down from the city, and my chauffeur can drive me all about the old spots — out to Fountain's Grove and all the lovely old places!"

Car, eh? Chauffeur? Then she did have a little money, perhaps a great deal.

"I suppose you married well, Nada," ventured Denton with more show of cordiality; persons with cars and chauffeurs, according to his reasoning, had money and little common sense — which were the kind of persons he liked to do business with.

"Yes, I suppose I did," said Mrs. Bascom, sighing. "My poor husband passed away some months ago. He left me in comfortable circumstances — quite comfortable, Mr. Denton. Sometimes," and she sighed again, "I wish he hadn't left me so much. It's such a terrible bother, you know, talking business and arranging investments and all that sort of thing. Oh, dear! I'll want to be renting a safety deposit box, too, Mr. Denton. I have considerable jewelry that I won't want to wear here, and some bonds and things."

"Certainly, Nada, certainly," said Denton, almost smirking now, and rubbing his hands together. A widow, a foolish, flighty widow, with money, who didn't like to be bothered with business; now that was the kind of customer Caleb Denton liked to have doing business with his bank! "I can probably be of a good deal of assistance from time to time, advising you as to your — er — investments. Your father and I were great friends, Nada — great friends. I thought a great deal of your father. He was a fine man, but — um — a little visionary — just a little visionary."

"I've heard father speak of you many times," said Mrs. Bascom, the sweetness of her tone giving no hint of the long-nursed bitterness which gnawed at her angry young heart.

By this time Denton had invited her behind the railing, motioning her to a seat beside his desk. She opened her reticule and drew forth a jewel case which she carelessly let fall so that the snap became unfastened and a dazzling little collection of diamonds, pearls, and other mounted stones showered over the blotter-pad.

"How stupid of me!" murmured Mrs. Bascom. And to himself Denton agreed that she was — but to him her stupidity meant tying up what must have been ten thousand or fifteen thousand dollars in these baubles when they could have been earning seven percent in wise investments.

Next came a prosperous little stack of bonds which Mr. Clackworthy had purchased for the very purpose in Chicago — rail securities, municipal bonds, and others of a more doubtful value. She placed them in the metal safety deposit box, but not before Caleb Denton had swiftly appraised their worth and knew that, regardless of her other possible holdings, the daughter of Louis Ramsey was worth at least thirty thousand dollars.

"Drop in and see me often, Nada," urged the banker. "You will be needing sound business advice, and I will look after your affairs just as if they were my own — just as if they were my own, my dear."

"Yes, I am quite sure of that, Mr. Denton," said Mrs. Bascom with great sincerity. "I feel sure that you would handle my money as your own."

Of course he could not be expected to fathom her subtle thrust.

III.

George Bascom, being for the purposes of the moment quite dead, was banished to temporary "widowerhood" in the city, but, two days after Mrs. Bascom's establishment in Liptonville, The Early Bird drove out in Mr. Clackworthy's sumptuous touring car which was to help Mrs. Bascom live up to her claims to riches. Mr. Clackworthy himself elected to remain in Chicago, where he directed the job of collecting Mrs. Bascom's debt from Caleb Denton.

"Say," demanded The Early Bird, when, in his chauffeur's livery, he reported to Mrs. Bascom, "had the boss let you in on the know? I couldn't get so much as a chirp out o' him. Do you think we're really gonna be able t' pry this bozo loose from any jack?"

"I don't know just what Mr. Clackworthy has in mind any more than you do, James," she replied with a smile. "In fact I am not sure that he has a definite plan. He's leaving a good deal of it to me, and I think that he will strike a course of action after I have found a lead for him."

"He's a wise gent," said The Early Bird in discouraged accents. "I admit that his head ain't a pretty thing t' feast the eyes on, but I'm tellin' the world that his old think-box is workin' on more'n one cylinder. An' the only way you'll catch that goof nappin' is t' administer chloroform."

Mrs. Bascom sniffed.

"I'll admit," she replied, "that Caleb Denton is a pretty smooth article for a nine-o'clock town, but when he starts swimming in Mr. Clackworthy's own private natatorium he's going to find himself in deep water with no life preservers handy."

However, as the days lengthened into weeks, Mrs. Bascom herself began to get somewhat discouraged. Nothing had happened. Banker Denton failed to display the expected vulnerable spot. He did, it is true, hint sagely of a certain well-paying stock which could be purchased at a good price, and Mrs. Bascom, recalling a previous incident in which Mr. Clackworthy had caused the canny seller of a worthless stock to fall suddenly into a panic and buy it back at a much multiplied figure, promptly sent this information to the master confidence man. But from his Sheridan Road apartment Mr. Clackworthy wired back a laconic "No."

"Pretty soft for the boss," grumbled The Early Bird. "Him an' that husband of yours sittin' around, takin' it easy, an' sendin' Nogo down t' the cellar for a bottle of the old stuff. Huh! Mebbe he'd like t' be stuck out here in this pocket-edition of a town, hearin' the crickets sing an' the dogs howlin' nights. The roarin' city fer mine!"

But Mr. Clackworthy evidently was not so idle as The Early Bird might have imagined. He took an office suite in the Meadows Buildings and forthwith there appeared on the door neat, gilt letters which announced: "The Excelsior Company." Beneath, in smaller letters, the additional word "Dyes."

Now it so happened — by Mr. Clackworthy's careful design, of course — that in Mrs. George Bascom's safety deposit box there reposed fifty neatly engraved stock certificates for the denomination, par value of one thousand dollars each, or a total par value of fifty thousand dollars.

Just when Mrs. Bascom was on the verge of sitting down and inditing an indignant note to the master confidence man she received a long, businesslike envelope which bore in the corner the conventional return address: The Excelsior Company, Meadows Building, Chicago, and within was a letter, also on the stationery of the same concern, which was crisp and to the point. It simply said:

DEAR MADAM: Find inclosed check for $6,000, our semi-annual dividend of 12 percent.

There was attached an entirely good and thoroughly spendable check for the six thousand, and also a brief note of instructions from Mr. Clackworthy which she mentally digested and destroyed. Then she made a trip to the Liptonville State Bank. Like a delighted child she approached President Denton and showed him the communication.

"Now isn't that perfectly wonderful!" she exclaimed in ecstasy. "All that money! And a cold blanket of a banker like you told me that it was a risky investment. All you bankers talk alike — mortgages at six percent! But the man who sold me the stock was such a nice young man; I just knew he wouldn't cheat a poor widow!"

Mechanically, perfunctorily, Banker Denton took the letter to give it a polite glance. When he saw the figures "$6,000" he stared at it more closely and with a growing interest.

"Semiannual dividend — twelve percent," he read. Of course it was ridiculous — dividends at the rate of twenty-four percent per annum! Yet it had been done. He felt a sudden wave of indignation that a silly, flighty woman should have stumbled into such a bonanza. Mentally he made a note that he would, just out of curiosity merely, make inquiry about The Excelsior Company which, as the letter head stated, dealt in dyes.

Mrs. Bascom banked the six-thousand-dollar check and went home.

And then Mrs. Bascom's healthy young bank balance began to dwindle. From its prosperous total of ten thousand dollars it shrank almost overnight.

"Great guns!" exclaimed Cashier Dinwiddie to President Denton. "That woman sure can get rid of money in at hurry. A few days ago she had ten thousand dollars, and now she's got an overdraft of a hundred and fifty. I guess it's all right to let her overdraw a little?"

"Yes, I suppose so," replied Denton slowly. He hated overdrafts. "Let me see her checks."

Cashier Dinwiddie brought in Mrs. Bascom's canceled checks. There were a few given to Liptonville tradesmen, one or two to Chicago business firms for goods she had bought, and the balance — nine thousand and fifty dollars — was made payable to G. Walter Ellis.

President Denton decided that he must speak to Mrs. Bascom; he didn't want to see her throwing her money away. He had better plans for it; with proper persuasion she might buy that Clement Manufacturing Company stock. Of course Clement was shaky, but he wasn't supposed to know that — nor was she.

Mrs. Bascom came to the bank that afternoon, to draw out more money.

"Nada," began Denton, "did you know that you were overdrawn?"

She wrinkled her nose thoughtfully.

"Overdrawn?" she repeated. "That means that I've taken out all my money, doesn't it? Oh, dear, how money does fly!"

"You are overdrawn a hundred and fifty dollars," said Denton severely.

"Oh, is that all?" asked Mrs. Bascom, laughing. "Goodness, you act like I had forged a check or something!"

"Banks do not permit overdrafts."

"But," she protested, "what harm is there in it? I didn't say anything when you had my ten thousand, and now you're making a perfectly awful fuss over a little hundred and fifty dollars! I think that's mean and unfair!"

Denton sputtered, outraged at this unbusinesslike heresy.

"I don't want to pry into your affairs, Nada," he said, "but — um — I am merely trying to protect your interests. I happened to be looking over your canceled checks, and I see one here for nine thousand odd. I hope you haven't been foolish."

"Oh, that's safe enough," she replied confidently. "That's only a little loan I made to — well; to the brother of a dear girl friend of mine. Such a nice boy he is, too! He has something to do with the market, I think. He needed a little money, so I just loaned it to him until — until the market changes, I think he said."

Denton groaned.

"Oh, why did the Lord give women heads!" he exclaimed. "They never use 'em. You've loaned a man nearly ten thousand dollars to buck the stock market. You know what that is? Gambling!"

"Oh, I'm sure it isn't gambling," protested Mrs. Bascom; "in fact he told me himself that it was a sure thing."

"Yes," said Denton, sneering, "that's what they all say."

But he knew better than to argue with women.

IV.

The Early Bird sat on the porch of Mrs. Bascom's cottage, his feet propped up against the rail in a very unchauffeurlike attitude in the presence of his employer. His face was clouded with gloom, but the impatient frown dissolved into a quick smile when, down the street, he saw "Snaps" Gentry, an almost half-witted urchin who carried telegrams for the local telegraph office in Liptonville, ambling leisurely toward them.

"Somethin's about t' pop," he said with satisfaction. "I ain't no prophet, an' my folks never had no luck with the ouija board, neither, but when I sees 'Rags-an'-tatters' hoofin' it this way I knows that the boss has quit messin' around with them high brow books long enough t' think a coupla original thinks an' give his attention t' the problem of sendin' out an S O S for a little soft mazuma."

Mrs. Bascom took the yellow envelope from the messenger and read it.

"You're right, James," she said, nodding. "I think today will tell the story."

Half an hour later Mrs. Bascom sat within the railing, beside President Denton's desk, a troubled frown between her eyes. Slowly she lay the telegram before the banker.

"I — I wish you would read that," she said. "It explains itself."

Denton picked up the paper and read:

Mrs. Nada Bascom,
Liptonville, Illinois.

    Must have thirty thousand at once to cover margins or lose all. Big bull market tomorrow. Will be either millionaire tomorrow or pauper. If you can raise the thirty thousand can save me. Will give you half. Don't fail.

    G.Walter Ellis.

Denton looked at her in scornful amusement.

"What is this, a joke?" he demanded.

"Joke!" she exclaimed indignantly. "Do you think it's a joke when one's very best friend's brother is going to be either a millionaire or a pauper tomorrow?"

"Do you mean to tell me that you believe any such stuff!"

"Believe it? Of course I believe it! Do you think G. Walter Ellis would lie to me?"

"Men have been known to do worse than lie when they were caught in the stock market," replied the banker. "They've been known to steal — and murder."

"But he is a gentleman — a man of his word! I don't think we'd better argue about it, Mr. Denton. The point is that I believe him, and that I must lend him thirty thousand dollars. He's really too nice a boy to be a pauper; it's terrible to be a pauper, you know. Will you lend me thirty thousand dollars, Mr. Denton?"

"Will I — what?" exploded Denton.

"Of course you will," she urged eagerly. "There are all those bonds and stocks and things in the safety deposit box. You can lend me thirty thousand on them, can't you?"

Caleb Denton suddenly thought of those fifty shares of Excelsior Company stock — shares that brought in a semiannual dividend of twelve percent. His eyes narrowed shrewdly.

"I am not so sure I will," he said hesitantly. "Are you sure you want to get the money?"

"Of course I'm sure!"

"Well, let's get your deposit box," he said slowly, "and I'll look things over. Maybe I will, and maybe I won't."

Mrs. Bascom's safety deposit box was brought in, and she unlocked it. In addition to the jewelry and the fifty shares of Excelsior Company stock, there was some thirty thousand dollars' worth of six and eight percent bearing securities.

Banker Denton shuffled them for a moment, tilting back and forth in his swivel chair.

"I am a little undecided just what to do, Nada," he said finally. "I never take snap judgment — never. You go out and come back in half an hour. By that time I'll have made up my mind."

When Mrs. Bascom had left the bank Caleb Denton summoned Cashier Dinwiddie.

"Dinwiddie," he said in a low tone, "call up the Consolidated Trust Company and ask 'em to give you the dope on The Excelsior Company; they're in the dye business. Ask them particularly about a semiannual dividend of twelve percent. And find out what the stock's listed at. I want a report in half an hour."

V.

When Mrs. Bascom returned in half an hour Caleb Denton was ready for her.

"Nada," he said, "I can't lend you the thirty thousand that you want — or think you want."

"You — you can't?" asked Mrs. Bascom in a tone of dismay. "Why?"

"It is — um — very difficult," said Denton, "to make people understand the peculiar financial situation that exists at the present time. Money is very tight — very. We have to be very, very careful — extremely so. Your security is all right for — um — normal times, but, just at present, it can't be done. Perhaps in a month, possibly in a week, but not now."

"But a week won't do," protested Nada. "I've got to have the money today. I've got to wire it to him. I've got to have it. I wouldn't disappoint him for worlds; I can't be responsible for making the poor boy a pauper. His sister and I are such good friends, and she would never, never forgive me."

"I know how you feel," said Denton, nodding and trying to put a kindly tone in his harsh voice, "but I can't lend you the money; of course if you've got to have it —"

Mrs. Bascom's face lighted with sudden hope.

"Oh, of course I've got to have it!"

"I might do something for you — um — personally. I'll tell you what. I'll buy your Excelsior Company stock outright — at par."

"But I don't want to sell it," protested Mrs. Bascom. "Why, I only got a six-thousand dollar profit on it a few days ago. It brings me in more than all the rest of my stock put together. I really couldn't sell it!"

"Suit yourself," said Denton, shrugging his shoulders with what tended to be indifferent finality.

"I — I've got to have the money," said Mrs. Bascom, apparently debating the question. "What — what would you give me for it?"

"Par value," replied Denton promptly; "a thousand dollars a share."

"But that's only what it cost — and it's making more money now than it was then."

And then Caleb Denton indulged in the most flagrant bit of deception that he had ever been guilty of.

"I couldn't pay you more than it was worth," he said, pointing to one of the certificates. "See there, Nada, it says right on the face of it — 'par value one thousand dollars.' How could you expect me to give you more than the certificates themselves call for?"

"I — I am afraid that I don't know very much about business," she laughed uneasily. "I — somehow I had the idea that it could be worth more than that."

"I have told you all that I can do," said Denton; what he neglected to tell her that stock with a dividend of twelve percent semiannually was worth a great deal more than par. "Take it or leave it," he added, "it's only a personal favor to you, anyhow, Nada."

"Dear, dear!" she said. "I just don't know what to do. I don't want to sell this nice stock, but — well, I can't let my best friend's brother be a pauper. Now, really, could I?"

"That's for you to decide," said Denton, smiling; it was the first genuine smile he had used in months. He knew what she would do.

"All right," she said weakly, "I'll have to do it. Will you give me a check, please, so that I can wire the money?"

And it seemed perhaps only natural that a young woman

handling such a big transaction should be unable to keep her fingers from trembling as she held in her hand a perfectly good check for fifty thousand dollars.

"My — my friend won't have to be a — a pauper after all," she murmured with a sly humor which, of course, was entirely lost upon Caleb Denton. If he remembered the words perhaps he realized the humor of it later, although it could never seem humorous to him.

VI.

The Early Bird stared at Mr. Amos Clackworthy in worshipful but puzzled admiration. From what Mrs. Bascom had told him he had tried to piece the scheme together, but he could not understand it. Even Mrs. Bascom was pleasantly dumfounded. In the presence of her husband, who had welcomed her on her hasty arrival from Liptonville, she had handed Mr. Clackworthy twenty thousand dollars.

Mr. Clackworthy, chuckling with that satisfaction which he always enjoyed previous to drawing aside the curtains and letting his coworkers "see the wheels go 'round," lighted a fresh perfecto as he turned to Bascom.

"And you, George," he said, "have the thirty thousand which your clever little wife wired to you. I trust, Mr. 'Ellis,' that you didn't squander it in foolish stock speculation."

For answer George Bascom who, via telegraph, had posed as the ambitious young stock plunger, tossed thirty one-thousand-dollar bills to the table in front of Mr. Clackworthy.

"Very good," said the master confidence man, smiling. "Your claim, Mrs. Bascom, against Caleb Denton, was, I believe, twenty-five thousand dollars. Correct. I shall take half of the fifty thousand for my time, trouble, and expense of collecting the same; the balance is, of course, yours. Quite a neat piece of work; you ought to be proud of your shrewd little wife, George."

"I am," said George warmly, "but what I want to know —"

"Yeah," grunted The Early Bird, "it's about time you was slippin' us an earful. I ain't figgered out yet whether you was just plain lucky, or whether Mrs. Bascom vamped old money-bags outta them fifty thousand beanos, or if this Denton goof went nuts at the right time, or what. Speak, boss."

"Yes," pleaded Mrs. Bascom. "I don't know for the life of me how you did it."

"Not nearly so complex as you would seem to make it," said Mr. Clackworthy. "It succeeded because Mrs. Bascom was a clever little actress. She convinced Denton that she had more money than sense, and that is the kind of victim that Denton prefers.

"Then we aroused his slumbering cupidity by making it appear that Mrs. Bascom received a six-thousand-dollar dividend check. A semiannual dividend of twelve percent will make even the most conservative banker's mouth water. Then Mrs. Bascom tried to borrow thirty thousand dollars. He preyed upon her seeming ignorance of business methods by clubbing her, as he saw it, into selling her stock outright instead of hypothecating it."

"But," put in The Early Bird, "you ain't tryin' to tell me that a wise guinea like old Denton is handin' out any fifty-thousand-dollar checks until he's give the deal the double-O?"

"Ah," laughed the master confidence man, "now we come to the nubbin of the scheme. I am quite sure that Mr. Denton, canny soul that he, is, did make diligent inquiry. Mrs. Bascom tells me, in her report, that he put her off for half an hour or so. Doubtless, Denton as I suspected he would, called some Chicago bank and asked about The Excelsior Company, dye dealers and manufacturers, asking them if it were really true that this Excelsior Company was declaring such stupendous dividends, and what the stock was selling at. If such was the case, the Chicago bank told Mr. Denton that Excelsior had really declared such a dividend, and that the stock was selling for over two thousand."

"Are you tryin' t' tell me that any bank's gonna be handin' out bum dopes like that, or did you forge some stock certificates of some real, fourteen-carat money-maker?" asked The Early Bird.

"Certainly not, James," reproved Mr. Clackworthy. "Your latter suggestion is ridiculous, for that would be dangerously criminal — forgery. I have committed no crime. I am entirely within the law.

"It so happens that The Excelsior Products Company is a

very lusty infant industry which has just capitalized some revolutionary dye formulas, and is making a mint of money.

"The stock in The Excelsior Company, which I myself organized — there was no legal bar to my using a similar name — is what Mr. Caleb Denton purchased. The fifty shares which Mr. Denton purchased represent the total capital stock, and since Mr. Denton is now the sole stockholder, and these offices are now his by all legal claim, suppose we go to my apartment where —"

"Where," finished The Early Bird, licking his lips, "there's a cellar with somethin' in it besides cobwebs."

MR. CLACKWORTHY'S PIPE DREAM

"AN observant eye, my dear James, often fattens the bank balance," philosophized Mr. Clackworthy as he and James Early, his co-plotter upon idle and surplus wealth, walked briskly along La Salle Street toward the city's financial district. "Only an opportunist can hope to be successful in our profession."

"You gotta cut out them chin gymnastics if you want me to get hep," grumbled The Early Bird. "I reckon you're aimin' t' say that the guy what drags in the kale is the bozo what keeps peeled for the yellow stuff, huh?"

"There have been times, James," pursued Mr. Clackworthy, "when you have failed to appreciate my interest in such a variegated assortment of subjects. Recently, for example, you offered strenuous objections to a little motor tour which we took through the State. Apparently I had given myself over to relaxation, but, nevertheless, I had a weather eye out for opportunity — and found it."

At this moment the master confidence man turned into an office building, and the presence of a crowd prevented confidential conversation. An elevator whisked them up to the fourth floor, where the pair stepped from the lift, and Mr. Clackworthy led the way around the corridor to an office, the door of which bore the announcement:

WILLIAM SACHS & CO.,
Stocks and Bonds.

Mr. Clackworthy was shown at once into Mr. Sachs' private office, for he was more or less a regular customer.

"Good morning, Mr. Sachs," said Mr. Clackworthy; "meet Mr. Early. I received your letter in the morning's mail, and I am here, ready to write you a check. You have procured the stock, I believe you said."

The broker nodded as he reached into his desk and produced a fat bundle of stock certificates. "There they are," he replied, fixing his customer with a curious stare. "Four thousand shares in the Stanton Natural Gas Co., par value one hundred dollars a share. That is the total issue with the exception of one thousand shares which we have been unable to find. My agents got most of it for one dollar a share, and narrowly escaped detention as lunacy suspects. As I warned you before, the stock isn't worth the paper that the certificates are printed on. Ordinarily, Mr. Clackworthy, I restrain my curiosity, but I wonder if you would mind telling me what you want with this worthless stock."

"I am buying it as an investment," replied the master confidence man with a smile; "you must admit that four hundred thousand dollars' worth of stock for four thousand dollars is quite a bargain."

"I admit no such thing!" exclaimed the broker. "The Stanton natural gas field gave out completely nearly ten years ago. The stock's worthless, and you know it. This five-hundred-thousand-dollar company was formed when the Stanton boom was at its height, and when it looked as if that district had enough natural gas to light every city in that part of the State. I happen to remember the details quite well.

"Some farmer around Stanton bored for oil, and, to his own surprise, tapped natural gas instead. One well after another was brought in, and it seemed that the supply was inexhaustible. This company was formed to sell natural gas to all of the artificial gas companies in cities within a radius of fifty miles, but about the time they had finished laying the mains the supply gave out. There wasn't enough gas left in the Stanton area to fry an egg.

"That's what you're buying, and you know it! You've gone into it with your eyes open. I warned you at the time you first commissioned my firm to round up this stock for you. Investment! Bah! You couldn't resell this stock for enough cash to get a shave! If you don't mind telling me, I'd like to know what the idea is."

"Investment," repeated Mr. Clackworthy enigmatically.

"But, hang it all, man, you don't expect the Stanton gas field to be revived, do you?"

"No, I don't expect that," admitted Mr. Clackworthy. "The

field is dead beyond all hope of rejuvenation. I don't ever expect to find any one fool enough to buy this stock."

Mr. Sachs threw up his hands. "You're too deep for me!" he exclaimed. "If you don't expect to resell the stock, you've simply thrown away four thousand, five hundred dollars, for I'm going to charge you five hundred dollars as our commission for getting hold of the shares. It was quite a job."

"Yes," agreed the master confidence man, "it probably looks as if I had thrown away some very good money, but I'm not in the habit of stinging myself in such an absurd fashion." He unscrewed the cap of his fountain pen and proceeded to write a check.

"Then you don't care to tell me what you propose to do with this stock?" urged the broker.

"I don't mind in the least telling you what I am going to do with it," replied Mr. Clackworthy. "I am going to keep it."

Mr. Sachs sighed. "Blamed if I wouldn't rather know what your idea is than to have the five hundred dollars commission," he said.

"And I would prefer you to have the commission," said Mr. Clackworthy laughingly, passing over the check and picking up the certificates. The broker stared at him intently as he moved toward the door.

"Either the deepest man in Chicago, or the nuttiest," he said under his breath. "Probably the nuttiest!"

"Boss," demanded The Early Bird, when he and the master confidence man were again in the street, "was that stuff on the level about the stock bein' N. G.?"

"For marketing purposes, James, its value is just that of old paper, an almost infinitesimal fraction of the coin known as one penny."

"An' there ain't no more gas under the ground near that burg than there is in a busted blimp, huh?"

"Mr. Sachs stated it very aptly, James, when he declared that there is not enough gas left in the Stanton field to fry an egg; there is no gas, and there will never be any more gas."

"Then, boss, watcha wanna pay out good dough for that bundle of pretty paper; that's what I wanna know!"

"It was my wish, James, to be in full control of the Stanton Natural Gas Co. and its assets."

"Unleash the chin, boss," begged The Early Bird. "I'm guessin' there ain't no assets."

"I suppose, James," the master confidence man said teasingly, "that it would not be amiss to say that I am, so to speak, indulging in a — well, a pipe dream."

II.

The Early Bird was not favorably impressed; in fact, he was utterly disgusted. He didn't like the looks of Kiethsville, Illinois, and so expressed himself, promptly, positively, and frankly. He had not gone four blocks on the way from the railroad station to the hotel when he began to wail bitterly.

"Honest, boss, you ain't expectin' to take any kale outa this burg?" he demanded incredulously.

"And why else would we be here?" retorted Mr. Clackworthy. "This is hardly the sort of place that one comes to for pleasure."

"You said somethin', boss!"

Kiethsville is on the northern edge of the big coal fields; it is a shabby, sooty place, made up largely of modest miners' cottages. When the six big coal mines, the profitable properties of The Plunkett Coal Mining Co., are in operation, every one is prosperous, for miners are good spenders when they have it. In the summer season, however, when most of the mines are running only one and two days a week, and some of them not at all, a pall of dejection hangs over the town. Merchants loaf listlessly in their stores and wait for the time when the public begins filling its coal bin.

The Plunkett Coal Mining Co. is but the corporate name for the Hon. Horatio Plunkett, who had, it was estimated, amassed two or three million dollars during the some fifteen years that he had operated the mines. In addition to his mines, he owned the Plunkett Trust Co., and was by far the richest and the shrewdest man in Kiethsville.

As soon as Mr. Clackworthy and The Early Bird had registered at the hotel, the master confidence man at once sent for an automobile at the public garage.

"I propose to spend about ten thousand dollars, James, during our first few hours in this charming little city," he announced. "I am now going to take you for a little ride and give you a look at my prospective purchase."

"Speak the piece, boss," pleaded The Early Bird. "Slip me the low-down. I ain't heard a peep as to why we're in this here junior Pittsburgh. Ten thousand bucks! Huh! I wouldn't give a hundred berries for the whole burg. Whatcha gonna give up all that kale for?"

"I am considering the purchase of a mountain."

"Say! Whatcha givin' me!"

"A mountain, James — a mountain of coal. Here's our machine; we shall now go forth and indulge in what is known as taking a look."

Mr. Clackworthy seemed quite familiar with Kiethsville, the result of a previous visit some weeks before. He directed the chauffeur to take them to the nearest of the Plunkett mines east of town. It was one of the shafts entirely closed down for the summer. The hoisting machinery was idle and silent, and only the pumps, which prevented the mine from being flooded by seepage water, were in operation.

"That's the mountain of coal which I propose to purchase — at least one of them," explained Mr. Clackworthy, and The Early Bird stared in puzzled curiosity at the sloping sides of the three-hundred-foot-high mound of coal shale some distance from the mine proper.

"I ain't jerry to this minin' business, but it don't take a very smart guy to see that it's the dump pile; it's stuff what's thrown away because it ain't no good, huh?"

"Precisely, James," answered Mr. Clackworthy. "At every coal mine is to be found a great mountain of coal screenings like that, growing year after year without hope of a purchaser; it is too compact and of such poor grade as to be practically without fuel value.

"This particular dump, I would say at rough estimate, contains some ninety or a hundred thousand tons of tailings, for which there is no market. I propose to buy it as well as others like it at each of the Plunkett mines."

"You're gonna give up ten thousand iron men for that worthless stuff; boss, are you sure that the old noodle is hittin' on all cylinders?"

"I should consider fifty thousand dollars as a fair price for all of the Plunkett dumps," said Mr. Clackworthy. "I am sure that Mr. Plunkett will be glad to accept, say, ten thousand dollars cash, and the rest payable later."

"But, boss, you've just said that the stuff won't burn!" protested The Early Bird.

"It has never been utilized as fuel," admitted Mr. Clackworthy, his eyes twinkling; "it is so fine that it smothers out a fire, and, as I said, the grade is very low. However, it's apparent worthlessness is just the point; it is my present job to buy a total of something like five hundred thousand tons of worthless shale — and make it burn!"

The master confidence man walked back to the waiting automobile, refusing to proffer any further explanation. When they had returned to the hotel, The Early Bird made himself as comfortable as his gnawing curiosity would permit, while Mr. Clackworthy went across the street to the imposing Plunkett Building, where Horatio Plunkett had his business quarters, and where were the executive offices of the Plunkett Coal Mining Co.

Mr. Plunkett's secretary, a thin, haughty little man who was exceedingly proud of his position with Kiethsville's richest and most important man, was accustomed to receive visitors with a chilling aloofness, but at the sight of the tall, prepossessing, elegantly tailored Mr. Clackworthy he found himself bowing. He decided instantly that it must be something very important, indeed, which would bring such a personage to Kiethsville.

"I am quite sure that Mr. Plunkett will see you, sir," he said in answer to Mr. Clackworthy's inquiry. He did not even ask the nature of the caller's business. A moment later the master confidence man was ceremoniously ushered into Mr. Plunkett's inner sanctum, a richly furnished office with a massive mahogany desk, expensively carved. On the wall facing the desk was a large oil painting of Mr. Plunkett himself.

Horatio Plunkett was florid and portly; an aggressive chin protruded from beneath a bristling gray mustache, and over a slightly bulbous nose were a pair of shrewd, cold eyes which had the habit of narrowing almost to pin points. A shrewd man, one knew instantly, and possessing a ruthless determination to turn his shrewdness into gold.

"What can I do for you, Mr. Clackworthy?" he asked in his booming voice, respectfully fingering the caller's impeccable card. His appraising glance darted up from the visitor's twenty-dollar shoes, along the lines of the hundred-and-fifty-dollar suit, to the pleasant face and faultlessly barbered Vandyke beard.

"I am about to surprise you," announced Mr. Clackworthy with his genial smile, yet getting to his point in quite a blunt, businesslike way. "I want to buy your six shale dumps. I am not a bargain driver, Mr. Plunkett; I will give you ten cents a ton."

Mr. Plunkett was surprised; more than that he was utterly dumfounded. The thin line of his mouth relaxed as his chin dropped in an expression of complete bewilderment.

"W-what!" he stuttered.

"I am both serious and sane," assured Mr. Clackworthy. "Your ears have not tricked you; I am offering to buy your six shale dumps for ten cents a ton; ten thousand dollars cash, and the remainder within a year. I have a bank draft in my pocket."

"What — what do you want with the shale dumps?" demanded Mr. Plunkett.

"I must decline to answer that question," replied Mr. Clackworthy. "You have six shale dumps which grow larger year after year and which are at present utterly worthless. They are without value to you; they are worth ten cents a ton to me, and if I can turn them into a profit, that would be my business. At ten cents a ton, your shale will bring you about fifty thousand dollars, which is just fifty thousand dollars more than you ever expected to get. Do we make a deal?"

"But, my dear sir, I have a right to know what you are going to do with that shale!"

"Not necessarily," returned Mr. Clackworthy. "I must have an immediate answer; if we cannot close a deal, I shall get the first train to Fallsburg, where there are other mines."

Mr. Plunkett's shrewd eyes searched the master confidence man's face for a moment, and he saw no signs of relenting. Swiftly he considered the possible uses to which the shale might be put.

"Do you intend using that shale for fuel?" he demanded.

"I prefer to keep my own counsel," answered Mr. Clackworthy, and Mr. Plunkett smiled in mixed triumph and sneering amusement. Experts had long since given up the problem of fuelizing coal shale.

"Humph!" he thought. "The fellow has a hare-brained notion that he can burn shale. Ten thousand cash! Even if he never completes the payments on the rest of the forty thousand dollars — and, of course, he won't — I'll be just ten thousand dollars ahead. If I don't get his money some operator to the south of me will." For a moment he continued to tap his fingers against the desk top.

"All right, Mr. Clackworthy," he agreed. "I'll deal with you — five hundred thousand tons of shale at ten cents a ton; ten thousand dollars cash, and forty thousand dollars payable in two installments divided over the year. Is that satisfactory?"

"Entirely so," said Mr. Clackworthy. "Call in your attorney and we will draw up a contract."

The contract was a matter of simple legal composition, and within the hour it was signed, and Mr. Plunkett had the ten thousand dollars. When Mr. Clackworthy returned to the hotel he found The Early Bird standing in the lobby, staring intently at a map of the State which hung on the wall.

"Boss," he said, "I just been givin' this here map the double O, an' it just filters through the bean that this burg is just twenty miles across country from the town of Stanton."

"Yes," admitted Mr. Clackworthy. "I believe that is so."

"An'," pursued James exultantly, "I ain't forgot that Stanton is the place where is them gas wells that ain't gassin' any more."

"Quite so," encouraged Mr. Clackworthy.

"An' you went an' bought up all the stock in that gasless gas company."

"Your deduction progresses, my dear James."

"I gotta first-class hunch that you buyin' this coal that won't burn has got somethin' to do with gas wells what won't gas."

"Proceed, James; proceed, and let us see just how closely you can hit the nail on the head."

"Hit it on the head, m'eye!" exclaimed The Early Bird. "How'm I gonna hit it on the head when I can't even see the nail!"

III.

Mr. Clackworthy could not remain long in a town without the town being gaspingly aware of his presence, and so it was with his presence in Kiethsville. He moved swiftly to the business in hand. The lumber company, for two thousand dollars of his money, had delivered large quantities of building material to a vacant plot of ground near the railroad tracks; a double force of carpenters were set to work, and a rough, shedlike structure, measuring some one hundred by fifty feet, went up almost like magic. When the carpenters went away, brick masons were put to work building a large oven along one side of the factory; then machinery began to arrive.

During these operations, Mr. Horatio Plunkett continued to chuckle over the bit of good fortune that had sent an unexpected ten thousand dollars his way. Since Mr. Clackworthy banked with the Plunkett Trust Co. it was a simple matter for the local magnate to know that of the original thirty thousand dollars that the stranger had brought to Kiethsville, only fifteen thousand dollars remained, and that, with Mr. Clackworthy's lavish check writing, this balance was dwindling. This seemed to Mr. Plunkett to indicate that his chances of getting another payment on his shale was negligible, but, well, ten thousand dollars was better than nothing.

It was one morning while Mr. Plunkett was considering these matters that Dawson, his secretary, entered and laid upon the desk a clipping from a Chicago morning paper.

"Here's what they are up to," announced Dawson. Mr. Plunkett saw that there had just been incorporated at the State capital, The New Era Coal Brick Co., Kiethsville, Illinois, Mr. Amos Clackworthy, president.

"Coal bricks!" exclaimed Mr. Plunkett. "Bah! Who ever heard of coal bricks! Don't bother me with such nonsense." Nevertheless, the coal magnate was possessed of a normal curiosity, and more than once he found himself wondering just what "coal bricks" were supposed to be. He was wondering when Mr. Clackworthy telephoned.

"Mr. Plunkett," said the master confidence man, "we are turning out our first coal bricks this afternoon, and thought you might like to come over."

For a moment the mine operator hesitated, but curiosity won, and he accepted the invitation. When he reached the shedlike factory, workmen were unloading shale hauled in from the Plunkett mines, and Mr. Clackworthy came forward with his genial smile.

"You are about to witness the production of our first coal brick," he said. "There you see your shale — worthless in its present state. In a few minutes it will be transformed into coal bricks which can be sold at the price of your best-mined coal."

Mr. Plunkett grunted skeptically as he stared about the unpretentious interior of the factory, if a shed could be dignified by such a name. Fires had been started in the big brick oven, and in the middle of the room was a ponderous machine with a big hopper and a cylinder with a capacity of about three tons of shale.

"Only one machine installed at present," explained Mr. Clackworthy. "It gives us a capacity of a hundred tons a day, but we'll expand. After we've cleaned up our profit on your five hundred thousand tons of shale, we'll step out and buy other shale dumps. Not much investment in factory, as you can see; not necessary."

"Humph!" grunted Plunkett. "What are you going to do with — er — coal bricks after you have — ah — manufactured them?"

"Burn 'em," replied Mr. Clackworthy. "Fuel on a par with your best-mined coal — cleaner and more convenient; and, as you doubtless know, ten cents a ton is far cheaper than you can mine coal."

"Humph!" grunted Mr. Plunkett again. He eyed the master confidence man closely, impressed despite himself by the brisk, sure manner and the confident voice. "I'll have to see it."

"And see it you shall," promised Mr. Clackworthy. "The shale is shoveled into the hopper and fed into a cylinder which is revolved under compression; that is our secret process. I can't show you the process, only the result."

Two days previously George Bascom and "Pop" Blanchard, two of Mr. Clackworthy's trusted coworkers, had arrived in Kiethsville. George was to be the sales manager and Pop was in charge of the factory. The latter, in overalls and jumper, was busy directing the workers when Mr. Clackworthy called him over.

"Mr. Plunkett, I want you to meet Mr. Blanchard, our mechanical genius. You may proceed now, Mr. Blanchard."

The hopper of the ponderous machine was opened, and it was shoveled full of dry shale; a cloud of sooty dust arose and filled the shed. The hopper door was closed, clamped down, an electric motor switched on, and the big drum began to revolve. The ground trembled with the heavy motion of the machine. Mr. Plunkett looked on curiously and stared questioningly.

"You are, I see, going to be much surprised," said Mr. Clackworthy. "As you know, of course, there is a certain amount of oil in all coal. Our process is merely to get sufficient excretion of oil from the shale to make it both readily combustible and cohesive. After the shale is taken from the machine you will see it sticky with oil; we mold it into bricks and bake it hard. The oil will make the coal bricks burn readily."

"Utter nonsense!" exclaimed Mr. Plunkett, but he waited to see the result. After some ten minutes the machine was stopped and the drum opened. The shale came out, moist and gleaming with oil. Mr. Plunkett, with a look of amazement on his face, picked up a handful of it.

"It — it's unbelievable!" he sputtered. "There — there can't be that much oil in shale."

"Yet there is; you have to admit that," replied Mr. Clackworthy.

"It must be a trick of some sort; what you've done is simply scientifically impossible!" protested the coal magnate. He strongly suspected that Mr. Clackworthy would presently draw him to one side and offer to sell him stock, and he was very much on his guard. He stepped closer and examined the machine; he had to admit that there was no conceivable place where enough oil to saturate three tons of coal shale might have been hidden. He looked about the factory; certainly there was not a secret nook or cranny in this barren interior.

The oil-soaked shale was trundled to the pressing machines and molded into blocks about the size of an ordinary brick; then the blocks were placed upon a shelved truck and rolled into the bake oven. Twenty minutes of baking and there was the finished product.

"Behold!" exclaimed Mr. Clackworthy. "The New Era coal brick!"

"Let's see it burn," said Mr. Plunkett skeptically.

"With pleasure," agreed Mr. Clackworthy, gathering up some wood shavings, kindling a fire, and permitting the coal bricks to ignite. Mr. Plunkett stared at the now blazing coal shale which burned with a ready and hot flame.

"High degree of inflammability," explained the master confidence man. "Easy to handle, no clinkers. Coal bricks should sell well, don't you think, at three dollars a ton, f. o. b. Kiethsville?"

Mr. Plunkett compressed his lips. He knew that the thing was ridiculous, and yet it was done. He sensed a trick of some sort, yet, confound it, there couldn't be a trick!

"You are offering stock for sale, of course?" he questioned shrewdly.

"Oh, no," replied Mr. Clackworthy. "We have too good a thing, and if our present plans go forward we can struggle along without outside capital. Quick sales is what we look forward to. The money will be rolling in soon, and that will give us the money to increase our production. We launch our selling campaign at once. Hey, George!"

George Bascom strolled over.

"Bascom, meet Mr. Plunkett — Mr. Horatio Plunkett. And, George, we will turn out our first hundred tons today, I hope. We'll have our first carload in Chicago tomorrow night and open up our display room the day following. Release those full-page advertisements in the newspapers, George.

"You see," he added to Mr. Plunkett, "our idea is to create a demand among consumers at once; that will start the dealers ordering."

"Humph!" grunted the coal magnate; his tone indicated the opinion that sales for coal bricks might not be so easy as Mr. Clackworthy imagined. He looked about the cheaply built factory again; again he sought for the trick. If the thing was on the square — and he began to admit that he couldn't for the life of him see how it could be otherwise — the cost of production was very low. He did a swift problem in multiplication and figured that The New Era Coal Brick Co. was about to realize a profit of a million and a quarter dollars on the shale for which Mr. Clackworthy had paid ten cents a ton!

Thoughtfully Mr. Plunkett returned to his ornate offices in the Plunkett Building and at once called in Dawson, his secretary.

"Dawson," he said crisply, "you and Jerry Hunt, the railroad freight agent, are good friends."

"He is Mrs. Dawson's cousin," replied the secretary.

"Good," replied Mr. Plunkett. "I want you to find out if this fellow Clackworthy has shipped in any crude oil. Find out for me to-day, if you can; if the thing is on the square — humph!" His voice trailed off musingly. "A million and a quarter profit — on my shale! Quick sales! Humph! We'll see about that; we'll see about that!"

IV.

If Mr. Amos Clackworthy had, as he had intimated to Mr. Plunkett, optimistic visions of an avalanche of orders for coal bricks, he was doomed to disappointment. Two thousand dollars spent in newspaper advertising had stirred no demand from the wholesalers or retailers in coal. But Mr. Clackworthy was far from disappointed. Keen analyst of human nature, he had anticipated this very turn in events. He knew that Mr. Plunkett was interested; he knew that he had put coal bricks through his laboratory and had found them high-class fuel. He had discovered, also, that Mr. Plunkett had blocked the sale of coal bricks; his agents had gone among the dealers, whispering warningly that they would find it to their advantage to "lay off" of coal bricks. It was broadly hinted that dealers who did handle coal bricks might find it difficult to get mined coal when they needed it most. It was a boycott, pure and simple.

Mr. Clackworthy sat in the offices of The New Era Coal Brick Co. and with him were The Early Bird, Bascom, and Pop Blanchard. The factory was deserted, for production had been suspended. Coal bricks wouldn't sell, so what was the use in making them?

"Well, my dear friends," began the master confidence man, "we don't seem to be a howling success, eh?"

"Coal bricks is sellin' like palm-leaf fans at a football game," grumbled The Early Bird.

"It's a conspiracy!" exclaimed George Bascom. "The dealers are scared to handle our product."

"Of course," went on Mr. Clackworthy; "that is what I was depending on."

"But," protested The Early Bird, "if them coal bricks ain't gonna sell, how're you figgurin' on gettin' a wise bloke like Plunkett t' cough up real dough for a factory what's shut down an' losin' dough?"

"My dear but sometimes dense friends," replied Mr. Clackworthy laughingly, "this is the work of Mr. Plunkett. He is noted in the coal trade for stifling the life of competition. He's trying to get us discouraged so that he can buy us out for a song. On my trip to Chicago yesterday I secured a nice collection of affidavits which give us the proof that Mr. Plunkett's agents have conspired to ruin us.

"Now, Pop, I think it's about time that you and I quarreled."

Pop Blanchard nodded cordially and leaned comfortably back in his chair.

"You don't like the way I have handled the business," went on Mr. Clackworthy. "You are demanding that I buy your stock. I have in the bank a balance of nearly five thousand dollars. I shall give you a check for it and you will turn over to me your stock. You cash the check and leave town this afternoon."

"Just as you say," agreed Pop good-naturedly. The Early Bird was about to demand explanations, but he saw from the twinkle in the master confidence man's eye that he would not have long to wait.

"That being settled," said Mr. Clackworthy, "I will now attend to a little matter of simple mechanics." He got a spade and a wrench which he carried into the factory. Winking at Pop, who, alone, seemed to be in on the secret, he began to dig a trench from the wall of the building to the big machine which performed the reputed function of extracting oil from coal shale. On he dug, without concern for his twenty-dollar shoes, and presently there was revealed a length of pipe. The Early Bird, watching eagerly, saw a great light.

The pipe led up through a hole in the platform on which the machine rested, entering the drum through a hollow space in the base, so well concealed that even a mechanic would have had a hard time figuring it out.

"I gotcha!" exclaimed The Early Bird. "That oil comes from —"

"From Stanton, of course," finished Mr. Clackworthy. "This is the old pipe line of the Stanton Natural Gas Co., which passes through Kiethsville on its way to Owentown. I was very careful to build our factory directly over a point where the old pipe line runs. The rest was simple.

"The pumps at Stanton were put in repair at a small expense. Our old friend, Jack Prichard, is over there with a mechanic. The gas line would carry oil as well as gas, and Jack has simply been pumping oil through the abandoned pipe line. When the machine was set in motion it opened a valve which permitted enough crude oil to pass into the drum to saturate the shale.

"I knew that Plunkett suspected a trick, and that he would move heaven and earth to find out if we had shipped in any oil. We hadn't, of course. Moreover, there wasn't a square foot inside this shed where a gallon of oil could be hidden.

"The oil made fine coal bricks, and the only trouble is that it costs about six dollars a ton to make 'em — about twice as much as we were trying to sell them for. Now you understand why I was not more heartbroken when we found it so difficult to sell our coal bricks."

The Early Bird wrinkled his brow thoughtfully. "Boss," he said, "mebbe you got this game all figgered out, but I gotta hunch that when Plunkett gets hep to the fact he's been stung —"

"I have considered that possibility," said Mr. Clackworthy easily. "I am ready to meet that emergency."

V.

For some days Mr. Plunkett had expected a visit from Mr. Clackworthy, and he smiled smugly when Dawson came in to announce him. As the master confidence man entered the local magnate's office his smile was missing, and he looked badly beaten.

"Mr. Plunkett," he said dully, "we're at the end of our string. Coal bricks won't sell."

A pleased chuckle sounded from the depths of Mr. Plunkett's throat, and he massaged his palms almost gleefully.

"They burn," he admitted. "How much are you out?"

"Thirty thousand dollars — every cent that I brought to this town is gone now. My bank balance is just twenty-one dollars. Blanchard threatened to throw us into the hands of the receiver; I know coal bricks are all right, so I bought him out."

"Ah, I see!" murmured Mr. Plunkett. "So you control the company?"

"I own ninety percent of the stock now."

Horatio Plunkett leaned back in his chair.

"I'll be generous," he said. "I'll let you out with a whole skin — thirty thousand dollars." As a matter of fact, Mr. Clackworthy had pinched out of his thirty thousand, including the five thousand dollars which Pop Blanchard had just drawn from the bank, a total of some ten thousand dollars. This made the expense of the adventure, including the ten thousand dollars paid to Plunkett for the shale, an even twenty thousand dollars.

"Ouch!" exclaimed Mr. Clackworthy. "You drive a hard bargain — too hard. I won't take it."

"Then you'll get nothing," answered the coal magnate snappily.

"I'll seek outside capital," declared Mr. Clackworthy.

"Seek is right," said Mr. Plunkett sneeringly. "Finding it will be the rub. Who will be interested when they find that the dealers have refused to have anything to do with your coal bricks, that your product has been virtually blacklisted?"

Mr. Clackworthy's body grew rigid with the pretense of great surprise. "So!" he exclaimed. "That's it? I begin to understand. Blacklisted, eh? Whose blacklist? I know the answer. You've worked a boycott on us; that means you must have wanted my company and wanted it badly."

Horatio Plunkett stared as he saw Mr. Clackworthy thus

transformed, and he realized in panic that he had been too hasty.

"Since I know that you really want to get your grasping fingers on my company, I guess I will have a little something to say about price!" exclaimed Mr. Clackworthy, triumphantly. "My price is one hundred thousand dollars cash. I'm letting you off easy, at that."

"You — you're crazy!" yelled the mine operator. "Fifty thousand — and it's my last word."

"I've got your number now, Plunkett, and I'm going to do a little squeezing myself. What an idiot you must think I've been! I've let you put over a neat little boycott on me. Coal bricks would have sold if it hadn't been for that; you'll clean up something like a million and a quarter as you figure it. I can't get capital, eh? Well, we'll see about that!"

For half an hour they bargained, and, finally, in his desperation, Mr. Plunkett raised his offer to seventy-five thousand dollars and Mr. Clackworthy, willing to give the magnate the feeling that he had triumphed, accepted it. Mr. Clackworthy went to the hotel for the stock certificates, and when he returned Mr. Plunkett had drawn his check. Reluctantly, as was his habit when parting with money, the coal magnate passed over the slip of paper.

"All right. I control the New Era Coal Brick Co. I shall take charge in the morning."

"I will be at the factory to turn affairs over to you," promised Mr. Clackworthy. He hurried out, for it was only a few minutes until the Plunkett Trust Co. would close, and he wanted to lose no time in exchanging Horatio Plunkett's personal check for a bank draft. It was so easy to stop payments on personal checks!

As soon as he had the draft the master confidence man found George Bascom and gave him instructions to catch the first train to Chicago to collect the money on the draft.

The next morning at nine o'clock Mr. Plunkett was ready to take over the factory, but Mr. Clackworthy reported from his room at the hotel that he was slightly indisposed, and he remained indisposed until he received a telegram from Bascom that he had safely collected on the draft. Then he telephoned to Mr. Plunkett that he was feeling better, which was true.

Thus it was that, a little after noon, Mr. Clackworthy and The Early Bird joined the coal magnate and the latter's mechanical engineer at the shedlike factory. The Early Bird was nervous.

"Look, boss!" he whispered apprehensively. "Plunkett's got a force of men ready; he's goin' to try an' make coal bricks."

"Of course," answered Mr. Clackworthy complacently.

"But, boss, he's gonna know in about two minutes that he's been stung."

"He is that, James."

"But, he — he'll have us pinched. Y' know, boss, I had a feelin' last night that the best thing I could do was t' sneak out of the hotel an' touch a match t' this dump. That would of covered our tracks; he couldn't of proved nothin' then."

"Arson is a reprehensible crime, James," reproved Mr. Clackworthy.

"We're ready," announced Mr. Plunkett. "As you see, I'm going to start production at once, and my engineer here will take charge."

"Here is the key," said Mr. Clackworthy. He waited as the workmen were put to work. At once they were instructed to shovel the dry shale into the machine while the engineer looked on doubtfully.

"You say you saw it done, Mr. Plunkett," he said, "but I don't see how. That looks like a converted concrete mixer to me."

"I saw it done," insisted Mr. Plunkett.

The motor hummed, and the big drum revolved. At the end often minutes it was stopped again, and the drum opened. Out poured the shale as dry as when it entered. Mr. Plunkett's face paled, and the engineer nodded an "I told you so."

"What — what has happened?" demanded Mr. Plunkett hoarsely. "There — there is no oil secretion. The — the shale is dry! What has happened?"

"I wouldn't say," replied Mr. Clackworthy, and he wouldn't, of course.

A horrible suspicion dawned upon the coal magnate, and he stared at the master confidence man and The Early Bird. James was having a hard time to disguise his growing panic.

"Fix that machine and fix it quick!" roared Mr. Plunkett.

"I only handled the financial end," replied Mr. Clackworthy. "I couldn't make a coal brick to save my life. Now if Blanchard were here —"

"Where is Blanchard?" demanded Mr. Plunkett.

"I don't know; he has left town," said Mr. Clackworthy.

"I think it must be a trick of some sort," accused the engineer. "That's only a concrete mixer with some fancy trimmings."

"Yes, it's a trick!" shouted Mr. Plunkett. "You are a crook! Give me back my draft for seventy-five thousand dollars, or I'll have you arrested. Understand? Your man Blanchard skipped out; the whole thing's a fake. You had some way of putting oil in that machine; you never did extract any oil from shale."

"You saw it done," reminded Mr. Clackworthy with dignity. "I dare you to prove any way that I poured oil into the machine. I dare you to prove that I shipped in a gallon of crude oil."

"Just the same your coal bricks are a fake!" cried Mr. Plunkett. "Give me back my money or I'll send you and that man, Early, to the pen. I'll have a warrant for your arrest in twenty minutes."

The Early Bird's face paled, but Mr. Clackworthy lost none of his calmness. The master confidence man stepped toward the office and motioned for Mr. Plunkett and James to follow.

"I thought you'd come across — you crook!" ejaculated Mr. Plunkett.

Inside the office, however, Mr. Clackworthy showed no signs of fear.

"Take a look at this, Plunkett," he said snappily. "This is an affidavit made by Gregg, one of your men. He confesses that you personally ordered him to carry on a boycott, and that is a Federal offense. Gregg is where I can find him, and I'll send him to the Federal officials if you try to get nasty. The district attorney doesn't love you any too well; he's been trying to get the goods on you for some time, for juggling coal prices and a few other things. Gregg's testimony will get you indicted by the Federal grand jury."

"You bribed my man, Gregg!" whispered Mr. Plunkett.

"We will not discuss his motives in signing this affidavit," retorted Mr. Clackworthy. "The fact remains that I've got the goods on you for a conspiracy in restraint of trade, of boycotting the goods of a competitor in an effort to make their stock worthless and buy in their company for a song.

"I'll admit that the machine doesn't work today; I'll even admit that it may never work. I know nothing about mechanics; to make the machine work is a problem for your engineer. You say coal bricks are a fake; you say I've flim-flammed you. Prove it! Prove, if you can, that I ever shipped a gallon of crude oil into Kiethsville. You can't do it.

"If you try any foolish move like having me arrested for obtaining money under false pretenses, your former man, Gregg, goes to the district attorney and tells what he knows. I won't give you back a cent; do just as you please."

"Buncoed!" gasped out Horatio Plunkett. He knew that he was licked. Mr. Clackworthy had him dead to rights; he had no proof that oil had been injected into the mixing machine, and Mr. Clackworthy had proof that would result in a Federal prosecution.

"Some day, you crook," he cried as he shook his fist in impotent anger and moved toward the door, "some day I'm going to get even with you for this."

The Early Bird sank into a chair and gasped for breath. "You — you bluffed him out of it!" he muttered. "I sure had a picture of the sheriff bringin' our breakfast in to us! You cleaned up fifty-five thousand dollars — a nice little piece of change t' split five ways, I'll say. Some — some little pipe dream! Boss, I gotta good one. Ask me — when is it that a coal brick ain't a coal brick? Ask me! This is rich!"

"All right, James, I'll bite."

"When — when it's a GOLD BRICK!"

MR. CLACKWORTHY TURNS CHEMIST

Walking stick swinging, Mr. Amos Clackworthy strolled leisurely along the cinder path in Lincoln Park; an autumn breeze, blowing landward from Lake Michigan, rustled the browning leaves and sent them sailing earthward from their branches. At Mr. Clackworthy's side, slowing his impatient steps to match the master confidence man's stride, James Early grumbled under his breath; to him a park was merely a place for band concerts and for children's picnics, not a place for poetic introspection such as he judged Mr. Clackworthy to be indulging in.

"'When the leaves are brown and sere,'" quoted Mr. Clackworthy musingly. "What a picture for an artist's brush! There is both beauty and sadness in the passing of summer, James."

"Yeah," mumbled The Early Bird disgustedly, "a guy gets t' thinkin' that a nice fat bundle of kale comes in handy when them zero winds begin blowin' in off'n that liquid cold-storage plant they calls Lake Michigan. I don't see you breakin' no speed records annexin' th' necessary wherewithal for you an' me spendin' the wintry day in Palm Beach."

"All in good time, James," promised Mr. Clackworthy, as he stopped beside the path and proceeded to make himself comfortable on one of the park benches. He produced one of his favorite perfectos from a leather cigar case and sighed in contentment.

"Boss, my fins is itchin' for the feel of some easy dough," stated The Early Bird, slumping down on the bench.

The two professional kidnapers of inadequately tended bank balances were seated near a lagoon, an artificial extension of the lake wherein the yachts and motor boats of Chicago's freshwater sailors were moored. Spanning this lagoon was a bridge high enough to permit boats to pass clear beneath it. This bridge was reached by a stairway at each end; its purpose was to allow people to reach the lake front without skirting the lagoon.

"The Bridge of Despair," remarked Mr. Clackworthy, gesturing toward the structure with his cane. "It seems to have been built especially for the convenience of those despondent folk who are too indolent to walk to the Chicago River."

"I don't getcha, boss."

"It's a favorite exit for those eager to leave this world of —"

"Aw, I gotcha," interrupted The Early Bird. "Guys what wanna bump themselves off, use it t' do a Brodie — huh?"

"Of course," pursued Mr. Clackworthy, "they could just as well walk across the bridge and wade out into the lake until they got over their heads, but there's something more alluring, I suppose, about leaping from a high bridge. Then, too, The Bridge of Despair has been rather well press-agented by the sob sisters of the daily newspapers."

"Believe muh," said The Early Bird, "the only way I'm gonna end my young life is mebbe t' drink myself to death — that is, providin' your private stocks hold out an' you don't get too blame stingy with the key."

Mr. Clackworthy sat erect with sudden interest. A young man had paused at the bridge stairway; he put his foot down uncertainly upon the first step, hesitated, and then started on. There was a dejected droop to his shoulders, and his face, even at the distance, showed itself grim and haggard. There could be little doubt as to his intention, and Mr. Clackworthy bounded forward impulsively.

"Come on, James," he called over his shoulder. "Here's a man who needs a friend — and quick."

At Mr. Clackworthy's call the young fellow paused in his ascent of the bridge stairs and looked around defiantly; no doubt he had expected to see a park policeman, for he seemed relieved.

"You dropped something," said Mr. Clackworthy with a smile, holding in his hand his own billfold, which he had swiftly removed from his pocket, first divesting it of all contents except a twenty-dollar bill. The would-be suicide stared stupidly at the pocketbook and saw the edge of the bank note peeping out one corner.

"I — I didn't drop that; much obliged, old man, but —"

"Certainly you dropped it," insisted Mr. Clackworthy as

The Early Bird, who had witnessed the master confidence man's bit of sleight of hand with the billfold, frowned in perplexity.

Evidently the desperate fellow was a man of keen perception.

"Mighty decent of you to offer me money in such a way," he said with a harsh laugh, "but the truth is that it'll take more money than the billfold can hold to see me out of my troubles."

"Been tappin' somebody's till, huh?" asked The Early Bird.

"How dare you!" exclaimed the other indignantly, thought of his troubles lost for a moment in his anger at this accusation.

"Come, my dear sir," urged Mr. Clackworthy, "let us repair to this park bench and discuss your dilemma; oftentimes, I've observed, a chap's apt to magnify his troubles under emotional stress, and they shrink almost to insignificance when they are given sufficient oxygen."

"My affairs are my own," muttered the stranger a bit haughtily.

"You better spill your sad story into the boss' ears," advised The Early Bird. "He's just nutty enough t' hand you a coupla centuries if he takes the notion."

"I have no wish to pry," said Mr. Clackworthy, "but it is possible that I may be able to assist you in some way." As always, the master confidence man "looked money;" in his faultless clothing, with his polished manner and neatly trimmed Vandyke, he looked the sort of man able to bridge almost any financial chasm.

The man just saved from a fatal plunge from The Bridge of Despair did not look the down-and-outer. His suit was expensive and nearly new; he wore a five-dollar cravat; his manners were polished and refined. He eyed Mr. Clackworthy thoughtfully for a second and then nodded.

"You don't look like a curiosity monger," he said. "I haven't any notion that you're going to be able to help me, but — Well, I'll tell you about myself, anyhow."

"That's the eye, pal," murmured The Early Bird; "let the boss in on the know. If it's the yellow stuff you need, the boss here is the guy that invented the recipe for makin' jack."

As the master confidence man led the way to the park bench he had so precipitately vacated, the stranger stared from James to Mr. Clackworthy, wondering how two such widely opposed types could be in each other's company.

"I hardly know why I should take you into my confidence concerning my troubles," he began, rather amazed at feeling the vague spell of Mr. Clackworthy's personal magnetism, "but there is something about you that inspires confidence."

"Too bad this goof ain't got as much in his pockets as he's got on his chest," murmured The Early Bird under his breath, "the boss could sell him the Northwestern Depot."

"My name," went on the stranger, "is Hugh Alexander. I have just lost my fortune — that is, it was a fortune to me. Fleeced out of it; flimflammed and buncoed out of my last dollar."

"Some con man had your name an' address, huh?" asked The Early Bird. "Speak the piece, bo; how was you trimmed?"

"Permit Mr. Alexander to proceed with his story in his own way, James," reproved Mr. Clackworthy. "To me the idea of fleecing a man of his last dollar is exceedingly reprehensible; a confidence man should never take more than his victim can afford to lose."

"Oh, you misunderstand me," protested Alexander. "The man who bilked me out of my money wasn't really a confidence man. He is a person of sound business standing."

"Often quite the worst offenders," observed Mr. Clackworthy.

"I refer," pursued Alexander, "to a man no less known than — Philander X. Bosworth!"

"The big money shark, huh?" exclaimed The Early Bird. "Yeah, I've heard of that bozo."

"You interest me; you do indeed," said Mr. Clackworthy with quickened interest, for it so happened that the name of Philander Xenophon Bosworth had long been written down upon the card-index file which the master confidence man, with businesslike precision, kept, showing potential contributors to his income.

"I am a chemist," explained Alexander, "a chemical inventor, so to speak. Some eighteen months ago I discovered the formula for a very valuable process of producing steadfast dyes. The discovery was so valuable that I conceived the idea of organizing a company. My own funds were extremely limited, and it was necessary for me to seek capital. Unfortunately — although at the time I considered myself very fortunate in getting the backing of such an outstanding figure in the financial world — I interested that darned old Shylock, Philander X. Bosworth.

"Green in the financial game, I fell easily into his trap. I let him get control of the stock. Of course I was at his mercy, but I would have realized something if he had played fair; but he wouldn't do that. Nothing would satisfy his insatiate greed except to squeeze me out — cold. I had a large block of stock and, of course, so long as The New Era Chemical Company, which was the name I gave it, had my dye formula, I felt assured of a substantial competence.

"The grasping old crook proceeded to freeze me out and clean me out. He inspired suits against our company, brought by other concerns in which he was interested. These legal actions were baseless, but he worked it so that judgment was obtained against us and my formula taken away from The New Era concern. He got our only real asset.

"I still had my stock, but it was worthless. He had the dye formula. I was flat broke. I've tried to get another start and failed. My original fifteen thousand dollars in capital is gone and — Well, I suppose it's cowardly, but I was willing to end it all."

Mr. Clackworthy lighted a fresh cigar, offered one to Alexander, and smoked thoughtfully for a moment; in this chance meeting there had been opened a way to have dealings with Philander X. Bosworth, an opportunity which he had long desired.

"Mr. Alexander," he said crisply, "you don't know a thing about me, so, to keep you from suspecting that I've broken loose from my keeper, I'll take you down to The Loop and show you that I really have some money. After that I shall offer you the amount of your original capital at the time you went into business with Bosworth; I shall tender you fifteen thousand dollars for your stock in The New Era Chemical Company, with the proviso that you aid me in certain ways."

"It isn't worth fifteen cents," said Alexander bluntly.

"Perhaps not five minutes ago," and Mr. Clackworthy smiled. "But I am thinking of present and — ah — future values."

II.

The Early Bird stared about the small office with a look of supreme disgust.

"Say!" he exploded. "This is sure a swell layout — not! Whatja do, buy the leavin's of some Wells Street secondhand joint?"

Mr. Clackworthy let his eyes wander musingly about the new quarters of The New Era Chemical Company; it was undeniably shabby and not at all in keeping with the lavish manner in which Mr. Clackworthy usually outfitted an office. Instead of the rich mahogany furniture and thick imported rugs to which he was very partial, the one room in a down-at-the-heel building on Van Buren Street was fitted with a few pieces of battered oak.

"It certainly is not prepossessing, James," the master confidence man said with a chuckle, "but, for that matter, it is not intended to be."

"What's the game, boss? I know you ain't adopted this Alexander goof as your pet charity."

"All in good time, James," replied Mr. Clackworthy. "Sh! Here comes Mr. Alexander now. Not a word to him of a 'game.' I think he has a strong suspicion that I have designs upon the surplus cash of one Philander X. Bosworth, and, while he is secretly willing that I should go the limit, he is one of those mortals who makes himself believe that he is very — ah — ethical."

The door opened, and Hugh Alexander came in. He had now entirely recovered from the depressed state from which Mr. Clackworthy had rescued him; he was in possession of fifteen thousand dollars, for which sum he had willingly but perplexedly parted with forty percent of the capital stock in The New Era Chemical Company.

"Well, Mr. Clackworthy," he said, "I see that the rejuvenated company is ready to do business, but for the life of me —

Well, I must say that your method of operating is most unusual."

"Mr. Bosworth must not be permitted to get the idea that the company is too prosperous or is blessed with any particularly bright prospects — at least for the present," said Mr. Clackworthy, smiling. "You see, Alexander, we want to buy a little of his stock, and we want to buy it as cheaply as possible."

"You're going to buy his stock!" exclaimed Alexander. "Why — why I rather got the idea that you were going to try to sell him the stock which you bought from me, although I couldn't for the life of me imagine why or how. I rather had the idea —" Young Alexander paused and flushed.

"You rather had the idea," Mr. Clackworthy finished the sentence for him, "that I had cooked up a scheme to unload the minority stock on Bosworth with some sort of hocus-pocus."

"Yes, that's the way I had it figured out," admitted Alexander; "I thought — Well, frankly, I thought that you were out to skin Bosworth in some way."

"You wrong us; you wrong us deeply!" exclaimed The Early Bird dramatically, with a wink at Mr. Clackworthy.

"Now," proceeded Mr. Clackworthy, "we come to the little service that you were to perform for me. I want you to go to Bosworth and buy from him just one hundred shares of his New Era stock. He now holds sixty percent of the stock."

"But if it's control you're figuring on," protested Alexander, "that only gives us forty-five percent. It will leave Bosworth fifty-five percent, with fifteen percent of it in the hands of Attorney Farmsley, whom Bosworth owns completely. That would not change the control."

"Ah!" murmured Mr. Clackworthy. "I see that you have learned a thing or two since you cut your business eye-teeth under Bosworth's tutelage. However, I do not want Mr. Bosworth to know that you have developed such a perspicacity. Listen to me carefully, Alexander, and follow my instructions to the letter."

Half an hour later Hugh Alexander left Mr. Clackworthy not quite certain whether his amazing benefactor was right in the head. He made his way over to LaSalle Street, where, in an imposing structure of granite, Philander X. Bosworth had his office.

Bosworth fingered Alexander's card for several seconds, frowning thoughtfully. He was a man of small stature, who made up in breadth what he lacked in height; from under habitually lowered eyebrows he glared ferociously out upon the world with greenish, calculating eyes.

"He's probably come to whine," he grunted out. "Well, the quicker I tell him where he gets off, the better. Show him in, Duncan."

But Bosworth was mistaken; there was nothing suppliant about Hugh Alexander's demeanor. The younger man calmly took a chair and smiled pleasantly.

"Good morning, Mr. Bosworth," he said cheerfully, although the forced cordiality of his tone almost choked him. "I called to see if you would sell me a hundred shares of New Era stock — at a reasonable price."

"What!" exploded Bosworth.

"I'll give you a thousand dollars for a hundred shares."

"What do you want with it?" demanded Bosworth, suppressing his amazement.

"I want control of the company," replied Alexander easily.

"It's bankrupt," declared Bosworth bluntly. "Besides, a hundred shares wouldn't give you control."

"Oh, yes it would," insisted Alexander, "It would give me forty-five percent of the stock, and Farmsley has fifteen percent. He's a good friend of mine; I'm willing that he should hold fifteen percent."

Bosworth smothered a smile. What a gullible child Alexander was! The fool had never seen through Farmsley's double-crossing, he thought. Even if he did sell Alexander a hundred shares, he would lack a great deal of having control.

"What are you going to do with the company?" he demanded.

"I'll tell you, Bosworth," answered Alexander. "You beat me in a shrewd business fight, and I was pretty sore at the time but — Well, it was business, and a fellow's got to take his medicine. I have a sentimental reason for wanting control of The New Era Chemical Company. It bears the name that I picked out myself; the company was part of me — it was me! I've worked out some new chemical formulas that I want to put on the market, and I'd like to do it with my old company. But of course I'd insist on control; I'm wiser this time. I would buy more of it from you, but I haven't got the money for that purpose; I need all the cash I've been able to raise."

Bosworth's shrewd brain carefully and swiftly digested the facts of the situation. It was, of course, entirely possible that the young chemist had worked out some new and valuable formulas; if he refused to give him what the idiot imagined was control, he would simply go out and organize a new company. If, on the other hand, he did sell him the hundred shares, Alexander might possibly give the bankrupt company a rejuvenated value. That meant that Bosworth, with Farmsley's stock, could still control and, if it amounted to anything, squeeze Alexander out, as he had before. Furthermore, if Alexander were merely nursing a dream, he would have a thousand dollars that he wouldn't get otherwise — and a thousand dollars was a thousand dollars.

Which process of reasoning was precisely as Mr. Amos Clackworthy had believed that it would be.

"All right, Alexander," Philander X. Bosworth said, nodding, "I'll sell you a hundred shares — for cash, of course."

III.

That day at noon when Mr. Bosworth dropped into his club for lunch, one of the first persons he saw was George Farmsley, the lawyer.

"Hello, Farmsley," grunted out the ponderous financier.

"Hello, Bosworth," returned the lawyer. "Just thinking about you; I picked up an unexpected piece of change this morning. You couldn't guess it in ten years, I sold — for actual cash money — my stock in The New Era Chemical Company. What do you think of that?"

Philander X. Bosworth's expression showed very plainly that he didn't know what to think of it.

"You — you did!" he gasped out. "Confound you, Farmsley! What did you do that for without asking me about it? Why, you big boob!"

Farmsley's mouth drooped open in surprise.

"What's all the row?" he demanded. "The stock's worth

nothing; you milked the company dry. Anyhow, it was my stock."

Bosworth sank, puffing and red-faced, into a chair.

"That Alexander kid tricked me!" he charged indignantly. "He pretended that he thought the stock he bought from me gave him control."

"Oh, you sold your stock, too, did you?" questioned the lawyer. "Then what in thunder are you kicking about if I sold mine? But I didn't sell to Alexander."

"I — I don't understand it," Bosworth continued, still puffing. "What does any one want with that stock? Who'd you sell it to?"

"Heaven only knows what they want with it," grunted out Farmsley. "I sold it to a man named — what was that chap's name? Oh, yes, I've got it now — a man named James Early."

"Never heard of him."

"Neither did I," went on the lawyer. "Don't think he had any great amount of money, though; we dickered a good deal about the price, and I think I got every cent out of him that he had. He seemed to be a most ignorant fellow, and I don't think he's in cahoots with Alexander; in fact, when I said that I knew Alexander pretty well, he asked me not to mention to Alexander that he'd bought the stock. I got the notion that he'd overheard some plan of Alexander's and was putting every nickel he had on a wild hunch that Alexander was going to do something with The New Era Company — which is more faith than I've got in it."

Bosworth sat up with a start.

"Confound it, Farmsley!" he exclaimed. "I've hit it now; the reason Alexander wanted control was just this — he's under a five-year contract to turn all of his chemical discoveries over to The New Era Chemical Company."

"Bosh!" snorted the lawyer. "He could get around that. All he had to do was organize a new company and put the formula in — if he's got one — under some one else's name."

"But Alexander's one of those conscientious chaps who wouldn't want to do a thing like that," argued Bosworth. "If he wasn't so stupid, and if this Early fellow hadn't asked you to keep mum to Alexander, I'd think that the young fool had worked us for control. Chances are that this Early had some inkling of what Alexander's discovery is and has sneaked in on the ground floor. Plague you, Farmsley, you had no right to sell that stock without consulting me! Now there's only one thing to do. You scout around and find out just what's in the wind. Do it this very afternoon. If Alexander's developed anything worth while, we want to know it. Look into this thing and let me know at once — at once, understand!"

An hour later Attorney Farmsley trusted himself to the doubtfully safe elevator of the Logan Building and ascended to the fifth floor. Around the shabby corridor he came to the shabby office of The New Era Chemical Company. As he entered, two men were seated by the window. They were Mr. Clackworthy and The Early Bird.

James, at a quick glance from Mr. Clackworthy, started up guiltily and edged toward the door.

"Ah," said Lawyer Farmsley, instantly noting The Early Bird's confusion, "we meet again, I see. I hardly expected to find you here."

The Early Bird gulped, seemingly unable to find words.

"Not quite so eager to keep our friend Alexander in ignorance of that stock transfer as you pretended," the attorney smoothly continued. "Acting as his agent, I suppose."

"I wasn't actin' as agent for nobody," mumbled The Early Bird. "Alexander don't know nothin' about it — yet. We was workin' on our own hook — me an' him." He jerked his head toward Mr. Clackworthy.

"Sh!" warned Mr. Clackworthy, finger to his lips.

"I seem to have run into a nice little plot of some kind," the lawyer remarked with a sneer.

"I told you not to come here, James!" exclaimed Mr. Clackworthy with a fine simulation of distress.

"Aw, I didn't know this bloke was gonna be runnin' in this-a-way," protested The Early Bird.

"Who are you, may I ask?" demanded Farmsley of Mr. Clackworthy.

"I am managing the office," replied the master confidence man.

"Oh, I see!" nodded the lawyer. "You're Alexander's employee, and you've gone in league with this other crook, here, to buy stock in Alexander's company on the sly. Nice, loyal way to treat your employer, I must say. Alexander will fire you when he finds out."

"I'm not particularly concerned about that, either," retorted Mr. Clackworthy. "Alexander is not paying me any salary to speak of." Which, as he was not getting any salary at all, was at least technical truth.

"I'll say he ain't," chimed in The Early Bird, hardly able to keep his face straight.

"And, speaking of crooks," pursued Mr. Clackworthy, "I've found out a thing or two myself. You're hand in glove with Philander Bosworth, and you helped trim Alexander before; I suppose you'd do it again — if I hadn't beat you to it."

"What's your game?" demanded Farmsley.

"I've got the stock now, Early and I together, and I don't mind telling you," replied Mr. Clackworthy. "I happened to discover that the fifteen percent of stock you sold this morning swings control of The New Era Chemical Company, the balance between Alexander and Bosworth. I can quite assure you that the man who gets that controlling fifteen percent from Early and me is going to pay a fancy price."

"Oh, I see; a holdup," said Farmsley. "You must think that Alexander has something rather good. A new chemical formula, I suppose?"

"Just that," admitted Mr. Clackworthy; "a substitute for gasoline."

The attorney started. He knew, of course, that chemists for years had been searching in vain for a gasoline substitute that would be cheaper than the refined product of crude oil. If Alexander had made this amazing discovery, it was worth a fortune.

"I don't believe it," he declared.

"Really, my dear sir," retorted Mr. Clackworthy, "I am not in the least concerned whether you do believe it or not. It is, nevertheless, true; a gasoline substitute that will cost very little. It is to be called 'Vegagas.' "

"Vegagas?" repeated Farmsley.

"Yes," and Mr. Clackworthy nodded, "a highly combustible fuel secured by the inexpensive process of cooking — vegetables."

"Vegetables!" exploded the lawyer, and then he laughed. "Either the whole outfit of you are crazy, or you're trying to make a monkey out of me. Vegetables! A gasoline substitute from vegetables — bah!"

"I would not believe it myself except that I happen to know that it can be done," stated Mr. Clackworthy. "Why, if you had your car downstairs, I could take a half peck of vegetables and five gallons of water and run your auto at least four times as far as a quantity of gasoline would take you for the same price."

"Rot!" snorted Farmsley.

"Wanna lay any jack that he can't take you, say, round The Loop on what he makes?" demanded The Early Bird. "I'll betcha fifty bucks."

"But — but it's impossible; it's silly!" sputtered the lawyer, rather stupefied by such confidence in these seemingly wild assertions.

"I'll betcha," tauntingly repeated The Early Bird.

"You're not stringing me?" insisted Farmsley. "You'll take half a peck of vegetables and five gallons of water and run my car?"

"Sure," said The Early Bird. "We'll show him, hey?"

Mr. Clackworthy hesitated.

"I am afraid that Mr. Alexander might object to this demonstration," he demurred.

"I knew it was a fake," charged the attorney.

"Aw, come on, gimme a chance t' get my mitts on this gink's fifty smackers. Alexander ain't gonna be back all day; he ain't gonna know nothin' about it."

"All right, I'll do it," consented Mr. Clackworthy.

"And I want a friend of mine to see it, too," added Farmsley. "I'll go down and phone to him. I'll buy half a peck of vegetables, too."

"We have some here; you need not bother about that," said Mr. Clackworthy.

"Oh, I guess not!" exclaimed Farmsley. "I'm not going to give you the chance to pull off any trick stuff; I'll buy my own vegetables."

IV.

When Lawyer Farmsley returned within half an hour he was accompanied by Philander X. Bosworth — which was much better luck than Mr. Clackworthy had dared to hope for.

"What nonsense is this, Farmsley?" he queried, puffing. "Vegetables! 'Vegagas' — bunk! I think the whole lot of you are nutty."

"I'll lay you fifty bucks, too, that the buzz buggy trots right along just like it was full of the real liquid," invited The Early Bird. "Are ya game? Put up the coin."

Mr. Clackworthy opened the door and led the two skeptical men into the adjoining room. In one corner there had been fitted up a gas stove on which was a ten-gallon copper boiler.

"You may put in the vegetables yourself," he said to Farmsley, and the lawyer did so.

"Vegetables!" exploded Bosworth for at least the twentieth time. "These two nuts are simply having fun at our expense, Farmsley."

"Well, they're paying fifty dollars to each of us for the joke, anyhow," answered the lawyer.

Mr. Clackworthy went to the corner with a five-gallon pail and, turning on the water faucet, filled the container. He carried the bucket back to the stove and emptied it into the boiler, after which he lighted the gas.

"Great guns!" sputtered Bosworth. "We're sitting here wasting our time with such tomfoolery. I'm not going to stay another minute; I'm hanged if I do. Five gallons of water and half a peck of beets and other garden truck! Huh!"

"And the secret Vegagas compound which is actually what does the work," added Mr. Clackworthy. "I'll put that in presently."

"What's in that — er — compound?" questioned Farmsley.

"That's the secret," replied Mr. Clackworthy.

The four men sat in restless silence for the space of more than thirty minutes when Mr. Clackworthy again approached the gas stove and emptied into the copper boiler a yellowish liquid. He returned to the window and waited for another twenty minutes, during which time he carefully kept his eye on his watch. There was something very confident in Mr. Clackworthy's attitude, and both Bosworth and Farmsley watched him with fascinated gaze.

"I think we can risk it now," finally announced Mr. Clackworthy. He turned out the gas under the open boiler and, motioning The Early Bird to assist him, carefully strained the liquid contents, still water clear, into the bucket.

"As every one knows," he said, "all vegetable life contains a great deal of alcohol, but heretofore its extraction has been prohibitive, due to the expensive methods of distillation. You have seen how this was done. You know, of course, that alcohol is the ideal fuel for motor cars, except for the prohibitive cost. We have here in this bucket something like five gallons of alcohol dilution which will run your car, as you will now see. Are you ready, gentlemen?"

"I don't believe it!" snorted Bosworth.

Together the four men descended in the elevator, taking the bucket of Vegagas with them. Farmsley's automobile was in front of the building, and he personally attended to the emptying of the gasoline tank and the pouring in of the other liquid.

"Prepare to fork over them hundred bucks," reminded The Early Bird as the lawyer got behind the steering wheel and touched his toe to the button of the electric starter. The starter whirred coaxingly, followed almost at once by the answering purr of the engine. The car was running.

"There was probably enough gasoline left in the carburetor to start the car; it won't run long after that water gets flowing," skeptically predicted Bosworth, who seemed to know something about motors himself. Nevertheless, he climbed into the front seat beside Farmsley.

"Let 'er hum!" The Early Bird exclaimed exultantly as he joined Mr. Clackworthy in the tonneau.

Farmsley threw in the clutch, and the car glided forward. He stared at Philander X. Bosworth, and Mr. Bosworth stared back at the lawyer.

"It works!" almost whispered the attorney in his awe.

"Half a peck of vegetables and a pail of water!" and Bosworth gulped. "You sold control in the company for a few hundred dollars! You — you fool!"

Farmsley did not deny it. On the car moved, block after block, the motor humming in perfect rhythm. The lawyer jerked his head around toward the tonneau.

"That pair back there," he whispered, "they've got that three hundred shares of stock I sold 'em, I think we'd better —"

"Yes," and Philander X. Bosworth gulped again, "I suppose we had — quick, before some one else gets to 'em. Drive to my office." He was silent for a minute; then he groaned and said: "I suppose they'll hold us up; they're a smart pair, and they'll make us pay — all because you let go of that stock. And we've got to get back control — we've got to."

Philander X. Bosworth proved a good prophet; he did pay. Two hours later Mr. Amos Clackworthy and James Early walked out of Mr. Bosworth's office, leaving the latter gentleman staring in deep pain at the stub of his check book. In Mr. Clackworthy's pocket reposed a check for exactly thirty-five thousand dollars which, deducting the fifteen thousand he had paid to Hugh Alexander and the cost of the stock, left the two plotters' bank accounts a net profit of a little less than eighteen thousand.

The Early Bird, still gasping at the swiftness and precision with which Mr. Clackworthy's scheme had been worked, and very much in the dark as to how it all had happened, lovingly fingered the proceeds of the two fifty-dollar bets which he had not neglected to collect.

"Boss," he begged, "slip me the low-down. So far as I can see that buzz buggy did run on the stuff that some guy recommends as a tonsil moistener. You dropped in a lot o' garden truck, turned on the water faucets, an' —"

"Oh, yes, James, the water faucet," interrupted Mr. Clackworthy, with a chuckle. "You see, that was a very peculiar faucet. Instead of being connected with the city water supply it was hooked onto a pressure tank containing — ah — alcohol, which looks a great deal like water, but hardly acts the same in the carburetor of an automobile."

"I gotcha, boss," and The Early Bird nodded. "Gosh, what if that stuff had of spilled out on the stove?"

"I am very much afraid, James, that in that circumstance

we would not have had such an easy time getting a thirty-five-thousand-dollar check from Philander X. Bosworth. I was very careful, I can tell you, to keep that bucket of 'water' away from the fire. As it was, our plan narrowly missed a catastrophe. While I was filling the bucket from the faucet, Mr. Bosworth lighted a cigar and tossed the match within a few inches of the running stream.

"And speaking of alcohol, James, it —"

"I gotcha, Boss," The Early Bird said, grinning. "I got a thirst like a camel."

MR. CLACKWORTHY
DIGS A HOLE

Being a man of naturally quick sympathies, Mr. Amos Clackworthy laid aside his book when he heard Nora's first sniffle as she went slowly about her task of dusting the handsome library of the Sheridan Road apartment. Nora was the Clackworthy housemaid; she had, true enough, been employed only recently, but housemaids were scarce enough to make their contentment a matter of concern, even had not the master confidence man felt a genuine interest in unhappiness anywhere he chanced to find it.

The Early Bird, sitting by the window, glumly watching the never-ending stream of automobiles which flowed past in opposite directions, glanced up hopefully as he heard the gentle thud of the closed volume on the table top; it give him the hope that perhaps Mr. Clackworthy would forsake the classics and devote a little of his time to the more exciting and far more profitable business of reducing the plethora of some swollen bank balance. But James' look of eager anticipation faded when he saw that the interruption had been occasioned by feminine distress.

"You seem to be in sorrow, Nora," said Mr. Clackworthy gently. "I have no wish to intrude myself into your affairs unwelcomed, but possibly there is some way in which I can assist you. You may feel free to confide in me."

These words of kindness swung open the floodgates of Nora's misery, and tears and wailing sobs burst forth.

"Great Goshen!" exclaimed The Early Bird, who always felt helpless and angry in the presence of a woman's tears. "Now look whatcha done! A guy as wise as you, boss, oughta know better'n t' sympathize with a lady. It's just like pourin' coal oil onto a fire t' put it out. Better stop her or th' tenants on th' floor below'll be phonin' to th' janitor that you've left th' bathtub t' run over."

Between sniffs Nora looked up indignantly.

"Don't mind James," consoled Mr. Clackworthy. "He

really is not as stony-hearted as you might believe; that gruffness of his merely is a thin disguise for a very tender heart."

"Heart!" wailed Nora. "Faith, Mr. Clackworthy, and it's heartless that this world is to — to a widder woman, t-tak-in' th' last cent of my savin's and my Michael's insurance money besides — o-o-oh!" And her sobs rent the air, for Nora was a woman of tremendous lung power. Mr. Clackworthy looked up quickly.

"You mean that you have been victimized?"

"I've been robbed — that's what I've been," she cried, her grief suddenly becoming nine parts of anger. "And wouldn't I like to get these fingers of mine on 'em!" The clenching of her big hands, strong, blunt, and muscular, boded evil for the subjects of her wrath.

She shook her head and sighed heavily.

"Sure, Mr. Clackworthy, and I'd be an ungrateful woman if I didn't thank you for your good intentions, but there ain't nothing you can do. Sure, and didn't I go to th' district attorney and tell him about it, and didn't th' district attorney tell me that they were the slickest lot of crooks unhung, but that they'd done it so slick and so legallike that there wasn't nothin' he could do. O-o-oh!" And the sobs broke out afresh.

"Just th' same," advised The Early Bird, who was of an extremely curious bent, "it ain't gonna do no harm t' slip th' boss th' lay an' let him size up these here porch climbers what —"

"Porch climbers, indeed!" Nora sniffed. "An' they weren't no porch climbers; I wish they had been. I don't keep more than forty or fifty dollars in my room an' that sewed up in th' mattress — an' I'd like t' see any porch climbers takin' anything from me!" The muscles of her shoulders swelled aggressively.

"James used the words 'porch climbers' purely in a figurative sense, Nora," explained Mr. Clackworthy. "James is extremely idiomatic of speech."

"Downright ignorant I calls it," muttered Nora. "He talks like a South Clark Street tough, so he does, an' for th' life of me I don't see what a fine, rich gentleman like you sees in him!"

The Early Bird colored.

"Tell me how you lost your money, Nora?" Mr. Clackworthy asked soothingly.

"It was confidence men that got my money — worse luck to 'em," explained Nora, and The Early Bird suddenly grinned behind his hand. "Hangin's too good for 'em!"

"Yuh hear that, boss?" said The Early Bird.

"I do hear it, James," replied Mr. Clackworthy calmly and without embarrassment. "And I thoroughly agree with Nora, for she is speaking of that species of evildoers who prey upon the credulity of people of small means. For this class of vultures I have nothing but supreme contempt; quite a different set, those fellows, from — um — others who — er — filch from those of wealth."

"I gotcha, boss," and The Early Bird nodded vigorously. "I'll tell th' world that you —"

Mr. Clackworthy frowned warningly, and The Early Bird subsided.

"I take it, Nora," pursued the master confidence man, "that you invested your savings in some fraudulent enterprise and have lost your money?"

"Yes, sir," nodded Nora. "I bought some oil stock — the Great Gusher Oil Company, it was."

"An' th' only gushin' done," ventured The Early Bird, "was by th' salesman what separated you from your kale. Them fellers is so smooth that they make silk feel like sandpaper."

Nora ignored the interruption.

"Th' stock certificates was all yellow-engraved, like real money," she went on. "They had pitchers of th' oil spoutin' right out of th' ground, an' they was so cheap, too — only five dollars a share. They told me that my two thousand dollars would make me a rich woman — they said it might make me a million."

"Barnum spilled a mouthful," apostrophized The Early Bird.

Mr. Clackworthy frowned thoughtfully.

"So you put two thousand dollars into this stock, Nora?" he asked. "Do you remember the men's names?"

"Two thousand, three hundred and sixty-five dollars; I should say I do remember their names!" cried Nora, answering both questions in one breath. "The tall, skinny feller with th' cast in his right eye was named Malone — an' a good

Irish name it is, too, for thievin' spalpeens th' like of him, I'll tell you. An' the fat one that had more oil on his tongue than was in th' oil well what they never dug, his name was Braddigan."

Mr. Clackworthy nodded.

"I do not know them personally," he said, "but I read of their operations; at the time an effort was made to have them indicted. As I recall, they played strictly within the law. They bought a tract of land on the edge of a real oil field down in Texas, purchased a broken-down drilling outfit and complied with all of the provisions of the law regulating stock-selling schemes. Their literature was carefully and cleverly worded so that legally not a single untrue statement was made. Legally, you and all of the other investors in the Great Gusher Oil Company merely took a gambling chance that oil would be struck. As I recall the newspaper accounts, some pretense at drilling was made — enough to comply with their prospectus and show there was no oil."

"Gamblin' chance!" exclaimed Nora indignantly. "Gamblin' chance, nothin'; didn't they tell me that they were sure to get a big oil vein; didn't they say —"

"Perhaps they did," interrupted Mr. Clackworthy wearily. "They always do, I suppose. Humph!"

He frowned thoughtfully and lighted a fresh perfecto.

"I would like very much, Nora, to undertake the job of collecting the money that you invested in the Great Gusher Oil Company," he said slowly.

"Ain't no use throwin' good money after bad," replied Nora. "I couldn't pay you; the district attorney said —"

"Yes, I know, Nora. The district attorney told you that you would have to charge it up to a sad experience and let it go, but — well, possibly the district attorney would not adopt the same collection methods that I would. Of course, I do not know that I can do it."

"Of course he can do it," said The Early Bird stoutly. "Th' boss ain't never gone after nothin' yet that he ain't put across. If them would-be con men wants t' get a few high-school lessons in th' skinnin' game an' asks me t' recommend a good but high-priced teacher —"

"Please do not interrupt, James," said Mr. Clackworthy.

"Nora, do you happen to have those stock certificates?"

"I've got 'em in my trunk," she said. "I was goin' to burn 'em up, but they looked so pretty and so rich with all that gold printin' on 'em, I felt like it was throwin' real money in th' furnace."

"Would you mind letting me look at them?" requested Mr. Clackworthy.

Nora hesitated a moment, then nodded.

"There'll be no harm in that, sir," she answered.

When she had gone back to the maid's room for the stock certificates, The Early Bird grinned expectantly.

"Gosh, boss!" he cried. "I'm hopin' that you do get th' old thinkin' machine goin' in high gear an' figger out a way t' throw th' hooks into these here bozos. Honest, boss, I'd be willin' t' donate a little of th' spare time of what we seems to have such a surplus lately t' separate them ginks from a bunch of their jack."

"Tut, James," reproved Mr. Clackworthy. "The laborer is always worthy of his hire; never hold yourself so cheaply. Should things so shape themselves that we find ourselves able to collect Nora's money, rest assured that we shall charge an ample fee for our services. Something seems to tell me that, after all, these two clever gentlemen, the Messrs. Malone & Braddigan, are not a whit less credulous in their way than the trusting grown children on whose slender funds they fatten."

"You're about as clear as this here Einstein goof's chin music about somethin'-or-other, but —"

"You mean Einstein's theory of relativity."

"But as I get that flock of words," went on The Early Bird, "there ain't none of 'em so wise but what some other homo can come along an' take 'em to a trimmin'.'"

"Crudely put, James, that is it," and Mr. Clackworthy smiled.

Nora returned to the room, the richly engraved stock certificates in her hand; even disillusionment had not entirely destroyed her admiration of their golden-hued printing.

"Faith, Mr. Clackworthy," and she sighed, "an' it's hard to believe that they ain't worth no more than th' meat paper that th' butcher wraps around th' roast."

Mr. Clackworthy took the certificates and studied them

thoughtfully.

"Capital stock, two hundred thousand," he mused. "As I understand it, Malone & Braddigan unloaded only about fifty thousand dollars worth of the stuff before they ran into a lot of unpleasant and unexpected publicity which put a quick stop to their operations. Humph!"

"You — you really couldn't get any of the money back?" quavered Nora. "I — I wish you could, sir; you — you see I'm not so young as I was an' — an' it was all I had. I —"

There was a touchingly eloquent pathos in her tone, and Mr. Clackworthy felt a sudden rush of sympathy for her.

"Nora," he said impulsively, "it doesn't make a particle of difference whether I do or not — I'll chance that. Here, take this fountain pen and sign over those shares to me, and I'll give you what you paid for them — dollar for dollar."

She gasped unbelievingly.

"Yes, I mean it," he assured her. "On second thought I think I'll have you sign them over to Mrs. George Bascom."

"You gotta hen on!" cried The Early Bird. "You've figgered out a way t' pull th' trick; you, an' George, an' Mrs. Bascom is gonna throw th' old harpoon into them cheap, imitation con men, eh?"

"I have a feeling, James," murmured Mr. Clackworthy with a shrewd twinkle in his eyes, "that the Messrs. Malone & Braddigan are going to regret that they didn't drill a little deeper than three hundred feet; I have an idea, James, that there is oil going to spurt over the top of the derrick on the Big Gusher land — just as is shown in the picture."

The Early Bird snorted disgustedly.

"I gotcha," he muttered with almost a sneer. "You've gone dippy over them pictures just like th' rest of th' suckers do. You've got th' oil fever, an' your temperature's ragin' around a hundred an' five. I ain't kickin' at you loosenin' up t' Nora here, but I draws th' line on sinkin' good coin into a hole in th' terra firma."

Mr. Clackworthy chuckled.

"Nevertheless, James," he insisted, "if you desire the pleasure of my company you will have to accompany me to Oilville, Texas. I think we shall start tomorrow; we will, of course, take George Bascom and his pretty wife along."

II.

The Texas Express thundered over the prairie country, and Mr. Clackworthy made his preparations to disembark, smiling teasingly at The Early Bird who gazed at him in disgruntled perplexity.

"Honest, boss," he protested, "I ain't made up my mind whether you're stringin' me, or if you've gone cuckoo. On th' level, boss, you ain't really expectin' t' find no oil; you ain't really gonna drill?"

"We shall certainly drill, James," and Mr. Clackworthy laughed, "and you will, I feel certain, enjoy the sensation of witnessing the sight of oil gushing over the top of a derrick — your derrick. I say 'your derrick,' James, because I have had Mrs. Bascom give you a few shares of her stock."

Occupying the other two chairs in the rear corner of the Pullman sat George Bascom and his wife, and they were almost as puzzled as was James, although they had long since learned that Mr. Clackworthy was not to be taken literally always. They felt that some bit of hidden shrewdness lay beneath the master confidence man's avowed purpose, but they were not obsessed by the same gnawing curiosity that troubled The Early Bird.

"The additional machinery which I purchased in Kansas City," explained Mr. Clackworthy, "should be along in a week or ten days. Mrs. Bascom has her instructions, and I will be in the next town where you can reach me over the telephone. I will run out to the grounds in a car now and then and help to keep things moving. I will be convenient when the moment of climax arrives — which will be when the oil starts flowing."

"But there ain't gonna be no oil flowin', an' you know it," stubbornly insisted The Early Bird. "Aw, boss, why don'cha let me in on th' know. As I get it, Mrs. Bascom here's gonna buy up all that Gusher stock an' —"

"Patience, James; patience," murmured Mr. Clackworthy. "Anyhow, I would not have the time to explain it to you now, for we are approaching my station. So long, folks; don't forget, Mrs. Bascom — do it just as I told you."

"I will," promised Mrs. Bascom, pouting prettily, "but just

the same I think you are mean not to tell us."

"Sometimes," replied Mr. Clackworthy sagely, "too much wisdom spoils the realism." And with this enigmatic answer, he picked up his traveling bag and made his way to the end of the Pullman.

After a momentary pause the train was in motion again, and The Early Bird fumed and fretted afresh.

"If I only knowed whether th' boss had gone batty," he said mournfully. "Sometimes I get th' hunch that he's really fooled that noodle of his into th' notion that he is gonna hit oil."

"Well," drawled Bascom, "I'll lay pretty good odds that oil or no oil, we're going to leave Texas with a good deal more money than we've got now."

"That's a cinch bet," laughed his wife. "When Mr. Clackworthy starts out to get anything he gets it."

"An' this time I got a feelin' he's gonna get it in th' neck," retorted The Early Bird gloomily.

Less than half an hour later the express stopped at the disreputable station of which even Oilville, which was not given much to pride of architecture, was heartily ashamed. An abandoned box car it was, for the railroad company had some time since discovered that a thriving oil town of today may be a deserted assortment of empty houses tomorrow.

One glance up and down the town's one street and The Early Bird's discontent was multiplied several times. James loved luxury, and the unpainted shack of a hotel gave no promise of it.

"I betcha we gotta wash at th' hotel pump," he grumbled. "I betcha they got cactus leaves for mattresses."

Oilville had not attained the prosperity of some of the other oil towns. It was some distance to the south of the fields where rich strikes had been made. A few wells, to be sure, had been brought in, but they were puny affairs, grudgingly giving a few barrels a day — hardly enough to reimburse for the cost of drilling. Somewhat to the northward there was considered to be still promise of future strikes and, as a result, hope had not completely died in Oilville.

But to George Malone and John Braddigan and their silent partner, Joe Paxton, it made not a particle of difference if every hole in the district was a dry one. They were playing the game a different way.

Malone and Braddigan were old-time promoters. They knew the game from A to Z; they had plied their profession before gold mines had given way to oil wells as the get-rich-quick bait for their practiced hooks. They were wise enough to play within the legal boundaries. They always purchased a tract of ground in the oil region and did some drilling. The stock selling and the drilling always stalled at the same time.

Joe Paxton, the silent partner, was president of the Oilville State Bank, and so silent a partner was he that scarcely a whisper connected him with the dubious firm of Malone & Braddigan. His duties were simple but extremely necessary. Malone & Braddigan were always being called upon for bank references and, for a third of the profits Joe Paxton would indite commendatory but careful letters of recommendation, stating that the Messrs. Malone & Braddigan had made large sums of money in the oil business, that they were substantial customers of the bank, and that he trusted them implicitly.

What he did not explain was the exact method of their operations, that why he trusted them was due in large part to the fact that he kept a close eye on them, and that they could not afford to double-cross him.

At present, as Mr. Clackworthy had discovered by adroit inquiry, Malone & Braddigan were in Oilville, following the unexpected exposé of the Great Gusher proposition and preliminary to another stock-selling campaign.

Malone, slight of figure and possessing in nervous energy what he lacked in bulk, was at a table in the back room of the Oilville State Bank, preparing the prospectus for the new oil company. It was careful work for the exact word shading in his glowing descriptions meant legal safety or jail. Braddigan, sleek, suave, portly, sat in a nearby chair, smoking as he critically studied his partner's composition.

"Great stuff, Malone," he said in a loud voice. "It'd almost make me buy some of the stock myself."

The door opened, and a trim, attractive young woman entered.

"I am looking for Mr. Malone, or Mr. Braddigan," said Mrs. Bascom. "They told me at the hotel I might find them here."

The two partners looked up quickly: it was not infrequent that they were annoyed by visitors who insisted on asking questions and demanding their money back. These scenes were always unpleasant, although not expensive. They had never established the foolish precedent of giving back invested money. However, one look at Mrs. Bascom's pretty, eager face disarmed any apprehensions. They always came in tears when they wanted their money back. And this young woman was smiling.

"Right this way, miss," called Malone. "This is Mr. Braddigan; I am Mr. Malone."

Mrs. Bascom took a chair and smiled upon the two partners.

"I came all the way out from Chicago to see you," she began, and the partners exchanged glances.

"I am a stockholder in the Great Gusher Oil Company," she went on calmly, and Malone began to frown forbiddingly.

"I have nothing to say," he said curtly. "We have no further connection with the Great Gusher Company."

"Certainly not; certainly not," agreed Braddigan. "We have nothing more to do with it."

"Oh, I am so sorry," said Mrs. Bascom. "You see I was so in hopes that — that I could induce you to go ahead with the drilling, for I have so much faith in Great Gusher — all the faith in the world!"

Malone gasped in speechless amazement and Braddigan dropped his cigar.

"You — you have faith in it!" stuttered Braddigan.

"Yes," answered Mrs. Bascom, "I know that there is oil — I know it! Of course, I haven't a great deal of stock — only a little over three thousand dollars' worth, but it's enough to make me very rich if we went on drilling and struck oil. And I do so much want to be rich! I didn't really buy the stock myself; my aunt gave it to me."

"What — what was your aunt's name?" demanded Malone.

"Nora Hayes."

The name was fresh in Malone's memory as that of a woman who had hounded him with unusual persistence before he got out of Chicago.

"That — that woman your aunt? And you have faith in the stock!" exclaimed the promoter.

"Yes, I know what Aunt Nora thought," and Mrs. Bascom nodded complacently. "She thought you were — were crooks, and that you cheated her, but — that's because she doesn't believe in dreams."

"Dreams!" breathed the two partners in unison.

"Of course, you don't understand," continued Mrs. Bascom, smiling. "Perhaps you, too, will think me very foolish but I dreamed of a great river of oil, and it was flowing right under the — the derrick isn't it — not far below where you first drilled. I dreamed it on my birthday, and every dream I have ever had on my birthday has always come true — always. That's why I believe in it so much. And that's what I came out here all the way from Chicago to see if I couldn't induce you to go on drilling again. Please tell me that you will; you won't have to drill very far."

The two promoters had experienced many strange things in their eventful lives, but never anything quite like this. They stared at the young woman in thunderstruck silence.

"Tell me you will," she insisted.

"But — but we haven't anything more to do with the Great Gusher Company," said Malone weakly. "We — we can't drill any more."

"Is that true?" she asked. "Or is it that you, like so many other people, just laugh at my dreams?"

"Well, I for one don't take much stock in the dream business," and Braddigan grunted. "But we couldn't do anything for you, anyhow; could we, Malone?"

Malone agreed that they couldn't.

"But somebody must own the stock," insisted Mrs. Bascom desperately. "The drilling must go on — it must!"

"I am afraid —" began Malone.

"Yes." She sighed. "I know what you're going to say — that no one will — will take a chance, I guess I had my trip for nothing, unless —" She paused and bit her lip thoughtfully.

"I wonder," she went on slowly, "how much money it would take to — to buy the control of the stock. I have a little money of my own — a few thousand. Now if it didn't cost too much to buy up the stock —"

Malone & Braddigan exchanged hurried glances; they still had one hundred and fifty thousand dollars in unsold certificates of the Great Gusher Oil Company. It was not, as they figured it, worth the match that it would take to set fire to it.

"I believe that — yes, come to think about it, Paxton, the president of this bank owns the stock — took it for debt. But it's only fair to you, miss, to tell you that I wouldn't advise you —" began Malone, hesitating between the impulse to pick up an unexpected few thousands and to answer the chivalrous urge which decried the fleecing of so pretty a girl. Braddigan coughed warningly; he had no chivalrous urge.

"I expect Paxton would sell the whole lot of his stock mighty cheap," amended Malone. "We couldn't get back into Great Gusher even if we wanted to because we are financing a new proposition which is taking all of our available capital — a new field which is, my word for it, the richest thing in the State of Texas."

"I wouldn't be interested in anything except Great Gusher," she said with great finality.

"I will speak to Mr. Paxton about it," put in Braddigan. "What would you be willing to pay for the stock?"

"I hardly know what to say," she replied hesitatingly. "You see, I didn't really expect to have to buy the stock. My husband and I — he came with me — had planned to spend all our money in drilling. I expect we will need it; I understand that it costs a great deal of money. I have only a few thousand —"

"Just how many thousand?" bluntly interrupted Braddigan.

"Only — only six thousand dollars," she answered faintly as if crushed by the knowledge that her capital was so pitifully small.

Malone and Braddigan exchanged glances and both nodded covertly.

"Well," said Braddigan, making a few figures with his pencil on the back of an envelope, "you ought to do quite a little drilling for two thousand; that would leave you four thousand for the stock. I don't know if Paxton would sell you all of his stock for that or not."

"But I wouldn't need it all," she reminded him. "All I would want would be enough to control the company so that I could call a directors' meeting and vote to go ahead with the drilling. You see, I have studied up on such things."

"I'll see what Paxton says," and Braddigan nodded. He went at once to the front of the bank where he held a whispered conversation with the bank president. In a moment he returned.

"Paxton says," he explained, "that so long as you only want enough stock to control and will leave him a block of it so that he'll be in on a good thing if you do hit it, he'll let you have it for four thousand."

"Oh, I'm so glad!" cried Mrs. Bascom. "I just know that you think I'm an easy mark and that I'm only giving my money away, but — well, I believe in dreams. I have the money in cash. I will want you to sign over some of the stock to my husband and some of it to his friend, Mr. Early, who is with us, so that we can hold a reorganization meeting right away and have a directors' meeting. We want to start drilling right away."

Malone went to the vault and got the stock certificates, thanking his lucky stars that he had not torn them up a few days before as he had been inclined to. It was but the matter of a moment to indorse them over. When Mrs. Bascom had tripped out of the bank, the two partners stared at each other in dumbfounded amazement.

"Talk about dreams!" exclaimed Malone. "Is this four thousand that I've got in my hand here or did I dream it?"

Braddigan chewed thoughtfully on his cigar. The oil business is full of strange happenings, shoestring strikes, and there is the germ of superstition in every oil man.

"Huh!" he grunted. "Wouldn't it be the very devil if she did bring in a gusher?"

III.

For months the solitary rig of the Great Gusher Oil Company had stood like a skeletonized tombstone to mark the grave of all the dead hopes that were buried in the yawning, cylindrical hole of the fly-by-night concern.

"Gosh!" murmured The Early Bird at the steering wheel of the ancient flivver he had purchased in Oilville as he turned to George Bascom and his wife. "There's Mr. Clackworthy or I'm a Hindu. He's been puttin' one over on us while we was moonin' around th' hotel waitin' for him t' give th' word."

"And he's got things moving, too," declared Mrs. Bascom, peering across the prairie. "He must have had the machinery shipped to Warrenton instead of Oilville, and trucked it out from there. Look; there's half a dozen tents up."

"I wonder what th' lay is," complained The Early Bird.

Ten days had now elapsed since their arrival in Texas, and the Bascoms and James Early, in accordance with Mr. Clackworthy's instructions, had twiddled their thumbs, so to speak, in the monotony of Oilville until his phone message that morning had told them to go out to the property of the oil company.

Mr. Clackworthy, looking not a whit less well dressed in his riding clothes than he did in his faultlessly fitting sack suits, strode toward them with a smile and an outstretched hand.

"Welcome to the Great Gusher," he said with a laugh. "It hasn't started gushing yet, but we'll have to be patient. Eh, James?"

"Yeah," grunted The Early Bird, "I'm as patient as a fan with th' score tied in th' ninth innin' an' a home-run hitter steppin' t' th' plate. Th' old bean's gotta regular pre-Volstead headache tryin' t' dope out this lay.

"Here Mrs. Bascom waltzed into town an' hands them two goofs, Malone an' Braddigan, another four thousand iron men, what added onto th' three thousand plus whatcha give t' Nora, makin' a grand total of —"

"Well, you must admit, James," and Mr. Clackworthy chuckled, "that even seven thousand-odd dollars is a small sum to pay for a controlling interest in a two-hundred-thou-sand-dollar oil company that is about to bring in a great gusher."

"Providin' it was gonna gush — which, take it from yours disgustedly, it ain't. Slip me an earful of th' info', boss."

"All in good time, James," murmured Mr. Clackworthy, turning to Mrs. Bascom with mock gravity and bowing.

"I welcome you as president of the Great Gusher Oil Company on your first inspection of the company's property," he said. "I regret, dear lady, that I shall have to deprive you of the pleasure of seeing the great well come in. The — er — dramatic climax, I fear, will compel you to be in Oilville at that moment. I will furnish you with your schedule presently."

The Early Bird, who had never been in the oil country before, wandered about curiously. Half a dozen workmen were at their labors. Already a giant metal tank had been put in place near the derrick, and three of the workmen, using horse-drawn shovels and scrapers, were digging out a vast hole.

"I guess I ain't jerry t' this oil business," he mumbled to Mr. Clackworthy, "but I gotta ask a few questions. What's that big tank for?"

"That's to store the oil in, James, when the well begins to flow," answered the master confidence man with twinkling eyes.

"Huh! A good-sized milk pail 'ud of been too big for that. An' whatcha diggin' that pond fer? I admit I'm ignorant, but I know dog-gone well they don't dig for oil thataway."

"I am employing a — er — novel method," and Mr. Clackworthy smiled.

At this moment the driller got the rig connected, started the donkey engine, and the chug-chug of the heavy drill thumping downward, biting its way slowly through the earth, began its monotonous monotone.

"The hole was already down three hundred feet," explained Mr. Clackworthy. "It's giving us a splendid start. However we'll have to drill through rock from now on and it's going to be slow work."

"Slow? Well I'd chirp!" exclaimed The Early Bird. "Th' president of Chiney'll be servin' you with an injunction t' stop boring a hole through th' floor of his capital 'fore you get enough oil t' grease a watch."

Mr. Clackworthy laughed gaily.

"James," he retorted, "your pessimism fools no one but yourself, and deep down in your heart you know that if I say positively that oil is to flow from this well, that it is to flow, and you would be the most disappointed man in Texas if it failed to happen."

The Early Bird grinned sheepishly, but refused to deny that he sometimes suspected that his idol had feet of clay.

"I should say," went on Mr. Clackworthy, "that the well ought to come in not later than a week from now. You, Bascom, have discovered that Malone and Braddigan will still be in Oilville on that date?"

"Yes." George nodded. "They're not to leave town until the first of the month. That's still two weeks off."

"Figgerin' on gettin' oil a week from now, huh?" demanded The Early Bird. "What day?"

"I should say Friday, James," and Mr. Clackworthy smiled. "But why do you want to know?"

"Well," mumbled The Early Bird, "I ain't really expectin' t' see no oil, but then on th' other hand, boss, if it does happen, I wouldn't wanna miss it."

IV.

"Culp was telling me that he happened to drive past the Great Gusher well this morning, and they're still drilling," remarked Malone with a puzzled frown as he glanced at Braddigan.

"Well, what of it?" grunted Braddigan. "It's her own money she's spending."

"But that's just the point, Brad," said Malone reflectively. "Where's she getting the money? She had two thousand left after buying that stock from us. She couldn't be drilling this long and feeding a gang of men on two thousand."

"Aw, that's easy," and Braddigan laughed carelessly. "She's a girl, and even oil drillers have a sense of chivalry — in Texas. I understood that she's way behind in her pay roll, but that the men stuck because she was a woman — and pretty. It's all over town about that dream business of hers; those drillers are a funny lot — superstitious as the devil. Like as not she's got some of 'em to half believe it. But they'll get tired of it pretty soon and quit. Say, wasn't that four thousand about the easiest pickup we ever ran into?"

"I sort of feel sorry for her at that," murmured Malone. "I understand she's sick in bed at the hotel — ill from exposure living in a tent out at the well."

"Maybe you want to give her back your half of the four thousand," said Braddigan sneeringly.

"Not on your sweet life, Brad," declared Malone hastily. "I can be sentimental — but not two thousand dollars' worth."

Both laughed and turned again to the printer's proofs of their latest prospectus. It was noon hour in the bank and President Paxton and his cashier-bookkeeper had gone home to lunch, leaving the two partners in the back room.

The telephone rang insistently. At first the two men ignored it, but finally Malone with an impatient oath got to his feet and walked over to the instrument.

"Hello," he cried.

"Hello, yourself," came the response in excited tones. "Take a message to Mrs. Bascom — quick. The — the well's just come in!"

"The — the what!" gasped Malone, his fingers suddenly trembling about the receiver.

"Can't you understand, dumb-bell!" shouted The Early Bird, for it was he talking, using the phone from one of the farmhouses between Oilville and the Great Gusher well. "Ain't this th' hotel I'm talkin' to? Well, you tell Mrs. Bascom that th' well's come in — pretty near blowed th' rig t' kingdom come, thousand barrels if it's a pint! Tell her right quick an', if she's well enough, t' come out here an' see it. Get that?"

"Ye-s, I — I've got it I—I'll tell her," replied Malone thickly, rubbing his hand dazedly across his eyes. He dropped the receiver onto the hook and, leaning almost lifelessly against the wall, stared into the curious face of Braddigan.

"Brad!" he whispered, "We've played the fool — you and I. That woman's well has just come in — a gusher — almost blew off the rig — thousand barrels if it's a pint — that — that's what he said. We — we've given away — thrown away — a — a million dollars!"

Braddigan leaped to his feet, overturning his chair.

"You're crazy!" he cried hoarsely. "You're crazy — or somebody's playing a joke on us. A gusher out there — ridiculous! We didn't even hit oil rock three hundred feet down."

"I — I know that, Brad," gasped Malone, "but — that's what he said. He thought he was talking to the hotel. He told me to tell her — that Bascom woman." He laughed harshly. "I guess I'll go and tell her — won't that be rich? Me, that sold her a million-dollar well for four thousand, taking her the news? Ha! Laugh, curse you, laugh!"

Braddigan got a grip on himself.

"Malone!" he cried. "We mustn't let her have it — and we won't. She doesn't know yet; we — we can buy it back. We've got to buy it back before she finds out. Call Paxton on the phone and get him right down here to open the vault. We've got seventy thousand in cash in there, but it oughtn't to take that much."

"Hey, not so fast," warned Malone. "I'm not going to buy a gusher till I see it gush. How do we know that that phone talk was on the square? The fellow might be a nut. I'm going to drive out there — now!"

"And let her get word in the meantime — a fine mind you've got!" shouted Braddigan.

"Just the same I'm playing it safe," retorted Malone grimly. "It'll be up to you to keep her from getting any news. Disconnect the telephone at the hotel; slip Bailey, the hotel keeper, a hundred if necessary — anything! I can be out there and back in an hour — and I'm going now!"

Malone's car was in front of the bank, and he tumbled into it. In a moment he was hitting it up the street at a good forty miles an hour. Almost more or less a furious driver, he pressed his heel against the accelerator and kept it there.

As he roared over Craig's Hill he almost lost control of the car as he gazed at the black cloud of liquid, the rich geyser, the like of which he had never before seen, pouring up in an expanding, rising, falling deluge over the top of the Great Gusher derrick — nearly a hundred feet high. Swiftly he computed that outpouring from nature's treasury as he jammed on the brakes.

"The biggest I ever saw!" he exclaimed aloud. "A good thousand barrels a day or I don't know oil from rain water!"

He did not need to go closer; he had found out what he wanted to know — that the well had come in a gusher. What counted now was speed — speed! He swung the car around and gave her all the speed she could stand.

Braddigan was on guard at the hotel entrance; one look at

Malone's thin, strained face was all that he needed to know.

"It's true!" gasped Braddigan.

"True?" repeated Malone. "Yes, it's true — and then some — biggest strike ever made around here. Has — has any one gotten to the woman?"

"Not a soul!" exulted Braddigan. "I've got it all doped out, and the money here in my pocket. We'll go the limit if we have to, huh?"

"Heavens, yes!" cried Malone. "But we ought to get it cheap enough at that — ten thousand at the most."

"Let's hope!" Braddigan murmured hopefully. "But a woman that can dream of a gusher before it's hit — well, you can't tell about people like that!"

"Rot!" snorted Malone. "That was just a coincidence. Let's be getting up to see her — and for Lord's sake get that life-and-death look off your face; you look too eager."

So engrossed were the two partners in their excited dialogue that they utterly failed to see the tall, elegant-looking man with closely cropped Vandyke beard who slipped into the hotel ahead of them. He was standing at the desk, pounding on the floor with his walking stick to attract the proprietor's attention, when Malone and Braddigan entered.

Mr. Clackworthy, for it was none other than he, turned quickly.

"Are one of you gentlemen the hotel proprietor? I wish to see Mrs. — er — Bascom who, I believe, is a guest here. Will you take up my card please."

And before either of the two partners could deny that they were the hotel proprietor, Mr. Clackworthy had shoved a card into Malone's hand. It read:

MR. AMOS CLACKWORTHY.
United Oil Company.

Malone developed a sudden case of palsy, and he gave the card to Braddigan. Braddigan stared at it, and his own face paled, but his wits had been trained to work fast in close pinches.

"Why, certainly, Mr. — er — Clackworthy," he said briskly. "Mrs. Bascom is ill, but I will deliver your card. Perhaps I had better tell her what you want to see her about. Being ill, of course —"

"You may tell her it is about the well she is drilling south of town," responded Mr. Clackworthy promptly. "I understand that she is in — um — financial difficulties and that — that I wish to make her an offer for the completion of the work. Our geologist reports — but I can take that up with her."

"All right, I'll tell her," said Braddigan with an effort at carelessness. "Going upstairs?" he added to Malone.

When the two partners got to the top of the stairs their perspiration was not due to the exertion of the climb.

"Heavens, what a narrow squeak!" whispered Braddigan.

"Heaven is with us — so far," replied Malone.

Braddigan had ascertained previously that Mrs. Bascom occupied the front room at the end of the hall. He rapped and a muffled "Come" answered him. The two partners entered the room to find Mrs. Bascom propped against her pillows, looking very white and ill.

"Oh!" she exclaimed in surprise, consummate little actress that she was. "I thought it was the proprietor's wife with a hot-water bag. I — I was not expecting visitors. I — can't you go away, please, and come back later?"

"I do not like to intrude, Mrs. Bascom," began Braddigan suavely, "but it really is very important, and — it's about the oil property."

"Yes?"

"Mrs. Bascom," pursued Braddigan earnestly, "I want to be frank with you. We are your friends; we have — er — much admired your pluck in going ahead with the well, and — um — it is with regret that we learn that you are not able to go through with it."

"But I am going through with it," Mrs. Bascom replied with spirit. "The men have been very good, waiting for their money, and —"

"Which is just the point," cut in Malone hurriedly; "the men at the well have served notice that they will quit tonight unless they get their money, so — we have come to you with an offer of assistance."

"You mean —"

"I mean," went on Malone, "that we have discovered

some — er — geological formations which lead us to believe that maybe your dream will come true after all — at least to hope so. Frankly, we were very skeptical — very! Now business is business, Mrs. Bascom. You are at the end of your string; your money is gone. We offer you the chance to continue the work; we gamble for big stakes — oil is gambling, you know — down here. Now here is our proposition. We will take back a portion of the stock which we — I mean Mr. Paxton — sold you and go ahead with the work. We offer you ten thousand dollars for — um — two thousand shares, that's the par value of five dollars a share."

"And that would give you — I mean Mr. Paxton, or whoever has the rest of the stock now — control, wouldn't it?" she asked.

"Perhaps it would; perhaps it would," agreed Braddigan, feigning carelessness. "At any rate it would make it about evenly divided. It really makes no difference, Mrs. Bascom."

She wrinkled her pretty nose thoughtfully.

"Very well," she decided, "since it makes no difference, I will sell you eighteen hundred shares — and keep control myself!"

Malone started to protest, but Braddigan trod wickedly on his foot, for Braddigan had thought of the shares that had been sold in Chicago; he knew that he could buy them in for practically nothing, and that Mrs. Bascom's apparent majority of stock would be no majority at all.

"Certainly, if you wish it that way, Mrs. Bascom," he agreed quickly. "Now if you have those shares handy, I will just give you the money, and we will close the bargain and not trouble you further about it. I am anxious, you know, not to have the men quit. Like as not they will drop some of the tools into the hole — they frequently do that out of spite, you know, and it would cost thousands of dollars to get the tools out; sometimes it means that the hole has to be abandoned entirely. Ten thousand is the price we agreed upon, so —"

"I certainly never agreed to any such price," replied Mrs. Bascom, smiling. "It seems to me that you two gentlemen are very eager — very. No, you'll have to give more than ten thousand dollars."

A board creaked in the hallway outside, but the two oil

men were too busy to notice it. It would have been extremely profitable to them if they had noticed it, for they would have been warned by seeing no other person than Mr. Amos Clackworthy, pseudo-representative of the United Oil Company, step to the window of a vacant room across the hall, walk to the open window, and wave his handkerchief.

At this signal The Early Bird and George Bascom, seated in James' dilapidated flivver which was almost hidden from view around the corner, started the car and drove toward the hotel.

"What — what would you consider a fair price?" asked Braddigan.

"And what would you consider a fair price?" countered Mrs. Bascom meaningly.

The pointed emphasis of the question convinced the two partners that they were dealing with a most shrewd woman; besides, time was too precious for jockeying. The representative of the United Oil Company, so they thought, was waiting impatiently downstairs and might be coming up at any moment.

"I would suggest — er — twenty thousand dollars," ventured Malone.

"I think I said a fair price," repeated Mrs. Bascom. "What would you say to fifty thousand dollars for eighteen hundred shares?"

"Ridiculous!" said Malone explosively.

"Out of the question!" exclaimed Braddigan.

It was at precisely this psychological moment that the noisy approach of The Early Bird's flivver, augmented by the combined shouts of The Early Bird and George Bascom, caused the two oil men to turn pale.

"She's in — she's in!" shouted James and George in unison.

Mrs. Bascom bit her lip to repress the laugh as she saw the consternation of the two bargainers.

"We — we'll give you fifty thousand," agreed Braddigan.

"But," replied Mrs. Bascom, "I didn't say I'd take fifty thousand; I just asked you what you think of it — and since you think so kindly of it, my price is sixty thousand!"

The two partners groaned, but nodded vigorously. However, Mrs. Bascom would not have felt quite so elated could she have known that in Braddigan's pocket was ten thousand more, and that he had been ready to go the full limit.

"Let's have the stock," said Braddigan, and Mr. Clackworthy tiptoed down the stairs, greatly pleased that he had such a talented trio of coworkers.

V.

It was two-thirty in the afternoon when Malone and Braddigan, eighteen hundred shares of Great Gusher Oil Company stock in their pockets, dashed out of the hotel, clambered into Malone's automobile, and opened up the accelerator, eager for a closer glimpse of the property which had so nearly escaped them. And at three-thirty, precisely the time when Messrs. Malone & Braddigan were praying for the heavens to fall upon them and the ground to swallow them up, and not quite understanding how it had all happened, anyhow, the Globe Hotel at Oilville lost three paying guests.

The Early Bird and Mr. and Mrs. Bascom, joined, of course, by Mr. Clackworthy, were making themselves comfortable in the north-bound flyer. The Early Bird shook his head hopelessly.

"I reckon I'm th' champeen dumbbell, anyhow," he declared; "but I ain't got all this lay figgered out yet. Of course I know th' boss ain't runnin' off an' leavin' no million-dollar gusher t' th' tender mercies of a coupla Jesse Jameses like them Malone an' Braddigan ginks, therefore th' ol' bean dopes it out that th' gusher gushed, an' yet it didn't. That's what th' boss here calls a pair of — what was that fancy word you used th' other day?"

"I presume that you mean paradox, James," and Mr. Clackworthy chuckled.

"Yeah. That's th' tongue puzzler I was thinkin' of. Come on, boss; th' curtain is rung down on th' last act as th' villains is seen weepin' an' wailin' an' gnashin' th' old molars, an' th' audience don't know no more than they did t' speak of than when you began playin' th' overture."

"A very artistic bit of work," murmured Mr. Clackworthy proudly. "I want to congratulate all of you, especially Mrs.

Bascom. But I am really surprised that James here has not seen through, since he speaks in terms of the drama, the chief 'prop' of the show. Here, let me furnish the key to the puzzle." He wrote:

Received from Malone & Braddigan	$60,000
Payment to Nora	$3,365
Payment for stock shares	$4,000
Labor at oil well	$1,500
Pump	$900
Pipes	$200
Reservoir	$400
Crude oil	$700
Total expenditures	$11,005
Net profit	$48,935

The Early Bird's eyes danced.

"I gotcha!" he exclaimed. "That big hole you was diggin' was filled with that there crude oil, an' at th' right moment you turns on th' engine and it starts pumpin' th' oil outa th' hole, an' up through th' derrick, just like a gusher. An' you shipped it into that other town in them big square boxes what didn't look no more like crude-oil containers than I looks like th' Siamese twins. I gotcha, boss; I gotcha! Ain't that th' lay?"

"I am forced to admit, James," agreed Mr. Clackworthy dryly, "that you have won a grade of perfect in your little problem in deduction, I promised you a gusher — and gave it to you."

"An'," The Early Bird grinned, "I gotta punk joke I gotta get out of my system. Speakin' of oil, that's what I calls a mighty smooth trick."

MR. CLACKWORTHY REVIVES A TOWN

The long-hooded car, its eight cylinders humming in rhythmic, mechanical perfection, rolled easily along the lake shore highway. On one side Lake Michigan sparkled like an amazing collection of jewels as the gently moving waves toyed with myriad sunbeams; on the other the greening fields extended, glorious in their new spring verdure.

Mr. Amos Clackworthy, host to his three coplotters, James Early, George Bascom, and George's pretty wife, sat at the steering wheel; he slackened speed that all might better enjoy the view.

"It's beautiful!" cried Mrs. Bascom. "Oh, why do we have to be cooped up in cities?"

"It is beautiful," and Mr. Clackworthy nodded, "I shouldn't wonder if even James, here, feels his thoughts stirred to —"

The Early Bird, seated beside the master confidence man, snorted indignantly at this accusation of poetic leanings.

"I'll tell ya what it stirs my thoughts to," he retorted. "Them fields is just the color of greenbacks, an' that reminds me that the firm of Clackworthy an' Company had better be discussin' ways an' means of grabbin' some kale instead of ravin' about the breeze blowin' through the trees, an' all that springtime stuff."

"And listen to that mocking bird!" cried Mrs. Bascom, squeezing her husband's hand. "Could there be sweeter music than that?"

"There sure could," mumbled James, although the question was not addressed to him. "Right now I'd rather hear a soup-spoon solo with Yours Hungrily renderin' the pleasin' ditty. The old molars is just achin' for the feel of a good T-bone."

"Now that isn't a bad suggestion," agreed George Bascom, who let his better half voice the poetic sentiments of the Bascom family. "We ought to get a first-rate meal at some of these country inns."

"Fried chicken!" exclaimed Mrs. Bascom, turning her enthusiasm to the suggestion. "Yum-yum! I can smell it right now! And biscuits!"

"Now you are spielin' poetry," said The Early Bird. "An' if the old peepers ain't foolin' me, I lamps what looks like a town over there t' the right. Le's go."

"I make the vote unanimous," Mr. Clackworthy laughed as he turned the machine into the side road along which lay the collection of roof tops which The Early Bird had pointed out. WARDSVILLE, ONE MILE, said a weather-battered signpost. A few minutes later the car was approaching the first of the modest little cottages. The yards of each were tangled with weeds, the windows of the houses vacant.

"Ain't no house shortage in this here burg," remarked The Early Bird. "All these places is as empty as a church on Monday mornin'."

The street through which they passed presented an unbroken line of deserted cottages, mostly cheap, hastily constructed affairs of three and four rooms. A little distance off there loomed, in dismal vacancy, a concrete block building. Evidently it had at one time been some sort of factory.

"Certainly a ghost town," commented Mr. Clackworthy. "Same old story; factory closed and the town died. We'll get no chicken dinners here, I'll wager."

The first sign of life was when a dog of doubtful lineage picked himself slowly from the middle of the street, too listelss even to bark at the strangers. And then they saw Sam Clark.

Sam Clark, as it afterward developed, was burdened by a multitude of public offices. He was postmaster, mayor of Wardsville, and chief of police, none of which duties took any great amount of time. When Mr. Clackworthy and his party first sighted Sam Clark he was sitting on the roofed over porch of the frame building which housed the post office. He looked up with mild interest and got slowly to his feet as the big automobile came to a stop. Plainly he was of the species *ruralis*; he wore a straggly beard; his shoulders were stooped, and his hands were gnarled by farm work. Perhaps that is why he looked so grotesque in his flashy clothes; he wore a loud, checked suit, sharp-pointed shoes, and flaming silk shirt, from the bosom of which glistened a diamond of not less than three carats.

"Lookey the rainbow!" exclaimed The Early Bird. "Solomon in all his glory sure was a piker alongside this goof. Lamp the sparkler, boss; some headlight, I calls that piece of ice!"

Mr. Clackworthy had, indeed, "lamped the sparkler," and he was puzzled. Expert that he was in the complex art of analyzing human nature, the master confidence man was somewhat at a loss to classify Sam Clark. It was a safe assumption that no man would thus array himself unless it be with the fruits of easy money — and where was there to be found easy money in this deserted, forlorn, weed-run village?

"We are looking for the inn," said Mr. Clackworthy.

"Somebody send you?" demanded Sam. Clark. It was to be seen that he eyed the motorists with appraising calculation.

"Our appetites sent us," Mr. Clackworthy said, laughing. "We are looking for a good dinner."

"A good chicken dinner," supplemented Mrs. Bascom.

"Yeah," affirmed The Early Bird, "we wants a bang-up feed."

Sam Clark scowled.

"There's an inn four miles along — on the east road." he said, as if he grunted out the words. "Turn to the right at the fork in the road down at the foot of the hill. Remember, now, turn to the right; the east road."

"We gotcha, Lord Chesterfield," chirped The Early Bird with an almost impertinent bow.

"Thank you so much!" Mrs. Bascom smiled sweetly.

Mr. Clackworthy darted another glance at the holder of local offices. One thing had swiftly impressed itself upon the master confidence man's mind — Sam Clark did not want them to take the road to the left! He threw in the clutch and the car rolled forward. He would not have been greatly surprised had he known that Sam Clark at once went to the telephone in his little office and cautiously advised of wandering strangers in the vicinity.

At the foot of the hill Mr. Clackworthy checked speed at the fork in the road, pointing the car's nose toward the left turn.

"He said the right turn, boss!" warned The Early Bird.

"So he did, James," and Mr. Clackworthy smiled.

"But you're goin' the wrong way, boss; this is the left."

"Quite right you are, James."

"Then what the — what the —" sputtered the puzzled James.

"I was created, my dear James, with a reasonably human amount of curiosity," replied Mr. Clackworthy. "I am, therefore, curious to find out two things: I am curious to know why our self-appointed guide back there in Wardsville was so eager to keep us off the left road, and I am further curious to learn just where that self-same man gets the money to array himself like a race-track tout who has just won a hundred-to-one shot."

The Early Bird's eyes widened in surprise, but he nodded vigorously.

"S-say!" he exclaimed. "Blamed if that bozo didn't look like real coin! You — you ain't figurin' on —"

"On taking our rural friend's diamond away from him?" finished Mr. Clackworthy. "Hardly that, James. No, just put it down to pure, unadulterated curiosity."

The road, winding through an avenue of giant trees, suddenly straightened out, and before them loomed the bulk of a big building which had "road house" written all over it.

"Ah!" exclaimed Mr. Clackworthy. "It seems that I was right. Here, a scant three-quarters of a mile from the heart of the village, we find our inn. There are ten, twelve, fifteen automobiles parked outside; that precludes any possibility that the place is deserted. The place is well patronized and, to judge from the makes of those cars, by a high-class clientele."

The Early Bird scratched his head.

"An' then what did that guy wanna try an' steer us t' a place four miles farther on for?" he demanded. "Mebbe he's knockin' this joint."

"That remains to be seen," replied Mr. Clackworthy.

They drove up to the side entrance, and the quartet alighted. As they stepped within an attendant frowned upon them with an amazing lack of hospitality.

"We would like chicken dinners for four," said Mr. Clackworthy.

"Fried chicken, of course," put in Mrs. Bascom.

The attendant frowned again.

"You made no reservations," he said coldly. "We never serve diners who have not previously made reservations."

"Come," and Mr. Clackworthy smiled graciously, "you are not going to turn away four well-paying wayfarers who are very hungry. Four chicken dinners, please."

"We shall be unable to serve you," again refused the inn's attendant sourly. "We have no chicken dinners."

"Then we shall have to eat something else," declared Mr. Clackworthy with unruffled suavity.

"Yeah," grunted out The Early Bird, "anything that an ostrich can use will suit me. Trot out the grub, old rain-in-the-face."

"I am sorry —"

"Come, my dear man," interrupted Mr. Clackworthy sternly. "This is a public inn, I take it. I want food for myself and my guests; I demand that we be served."

Mr. Clackworthy could be very compelling when he chose, and he fixed the servant's stubborn gaze with an eye that commanded obedience.

"I — I might manage to get you sandwiches; something very light," he capitulated. "I will show you to the dining room."

In the dining room, Mr. Clackworthy, The Early Bird, and the Bascoms found themselves the sole diners.

"Wonder where all them swells what's got their cars parked out in front is munchin' their cud," murmured The Early Bird. "There's somethin' queer about this joint."

"It's uncanny, isn't it?" and Mrs. Bascom shivered. "What do you make of it, Mr. Clackworthy?"

"I have my suspicions," said the master confidence man with a smile. "Can't you guess?"

"Is — is it some sort of a — a criminal's hangout?" she demanded breathlessly.

"It depends, my dear friends, just what you mean by the word 'criminal.' If you mean in the strictly technical sense — yes. Really you ought to size it up with half an eye. Do you get it, James?"

"Just like I get this here Einstein goof's line of chatter,

boss."

A moment later the surly servant came in with sandwiches; certainly if he were deliberately discouraging them from becoming future patrons, he was choosing a generally approved way of driving away trade. He almost slung the food in front of Mr. Clackworthy, tipped over Mrs. Bascom's coffee, and glared at all four. The sandwiches were sorry, inadequate things.

"Come, my dear man," chidingly said Mr. Clackworthy, "we can not really be such unwelcome guests as you seem to imagine."

"Sir?"

"Do we look like detectives?"

"Sir?"

"We, my friends and I," continued Mr. Clackworthy calmly, "would like to be permitted to join your other guests upstairs."

The servant seemed momentarily disconcerted.

"You are mistaken," he said frigidly. "There are no guests upstairs." And he stalked away.

The Early Bird leaned forward eagerly.

"Slip me the lay, boss," he pleaded.

"Yes, please do," urged Mrs. Bascom, and George, her husband, nodded to indicate his own curiosity.

"Above this ceiling," explained Mr. Clackworthy, "there is a place of which I vaguely remember having heard — a sort of exclusive Monte Carlo where the rich of the big city in which we live come to win the excitement which is to be gotten at the roulette wheel."

"A gamblin' joint, eh, boss?" cried The Early Bird.

"Oh, my dear James, not a gambling joint!" exclaimed Mr. Clackworthy in mock horror. "A gambling establishment; a place where those of great means can come in safety and quiet and gamble to their heart's content without fear of detection. A card of admission by previous arrangement is necessary, as all of us have been forced to observe. And —"

Mr. Clackworthy's eyes narrowed thoughtfully, and he drummed his long fingers on the tablecloth as a sudden idea took possession of him.

"And," he went on slowly, "for this rudeness to you and to

myself, my three dear friends, I am determined to collect a sum of money adequate for our — er — our wounded pride. How much balm is necessary to soothe your ruffled feelings, James?"

"Huh!" grunted James. "If that dumb-bell will come back here an' give me a real slice of ham t' put between these two pieces of bread, an' trot out the mustard bottle, I'll let him off for a coupla bucks. Ferget it, boss; these ginks is wise ones. The percentage is always on their side."

Mrs. Bascom took the master confidence man's remarks as genial raillery.

"I certainly think that the loss of a good chicken dinner is worth five thousand dollars." And she laughed.

"That would be a twenty-thousand total for the four of us," Mr. Clackworthy said. "Then we must add something for the expenses of collection. Suppose we make it twenty-five thousand dollars in all."

"Boss!" sputtered The Early Bird. "You ain't on the square with that twenty-five-thousand-dollar stuff?"

"I certainly am, James."

"How ya gonna do it?"

"Of that, James, I am not so sure," admitted Mr. Clackworthy, "but I begin to get the dawning of an idea. One thing, however, is certain; we're going to get the money."

II.

Two weeks had passed, and The Early Bird, mooning disconsolately in Mr. Clackworthy's Sheridan Road apartment, chafing under the protracted inaction, had quite forgotten about the master confidence man's threat to reduce the doubtless swollen profits of Chicago's suburban Monte Carlo; he had, in fact, dismissed it as an idle promise of vengeance, made in a moment of indignation. Therefore James was startled when the "boss," smiling his teasing smile, revived the subject.

"James," said Mr. Clackworthy, "I wish that you would give our good friend, George Bascom, a ring, and tell him that he and his wife are invited to be ready at two o'clock this afternoon for a trip to Wardsville. Mrs. Bascom should take her trunk along; we will be there for some time.

"Wardsville?" questioned The Early Bird; then his brow cleared. "Y' mean that burg out north sufferin' from the sleepin' sickness?"

"Precisely the place, James, and your metaphor is very apt; we are about to awaken Wardsville from its somnambulism."

"Whatever that means," grumbled The Early Bird. "Translate it into my language, boss. Y' mean you're gonna throw the hooks into the outfit that's runnin' that gilt-edge speak-easy? Y' gonna lift the sparkler off'n that over-dressed hick what we seen flaggin' unwelcome customers?"

"Some of the sort, James," and Mr. Clackworthy laughed, "except, however, that I have no designs upon Mr. Sam Clark's jewelry — his name is Sam Clark, you know, and he is mayor of Wardsville, police officer, and postmaster. However, I am about to interfere seriously with the revenue which purchased Mr. Clark's raiment and precious stones. Call the Bascoms, please; two o'clock is the hour I shall call for them."

"Aw, boss, ain'tcha gonna slip me an earful?"

"Not at present, old dear. I reserve the dramatist's right to withhold the suspense."

And The Early Bird, grumbling, went to the telephone.

As they made the trip to Wardsville it was evident to the Bascoms as well as to James Early that the master confidence man had prepared a genuine surprise for them, for Mr. Clackworthy was in his best humor, jovial and joking and teasingly warding off the eager questions of his three puzzled coworkers. As the car entered the outskirts of the town it was evident, too, that a transformation was taking place. Wholesale war had been declared on the wilderness of weeds, and, as they stopped at one of the larger cottages, there was evidence of occupancy.

"How do you like it?" asked Mr. Clackworthy of Mrs. Bascom.

"It's quite pretty," she replied, "but it needs a good many things done to it — flowers and things like that."

"You think, then, that you can endure living here the rest of the summer?" pursued Mr. Clackworthy.

"Live here — me?" she gasped. "The rest of the summer?

You're joking!"

"Indeed I am not," he replied. "This is the first little sur-prise for you; this is the place that I've fixed up for you and George. You'll find it fairly cozy, although hardly so elaborate as you might desire — if it were to be your permanent resi-dence."

The Early Bird was blinking rapidly as he tried to fathom the depths of what was evidently an intricate scheme whereby Mr. Clackworthy planned to annex to his own bank account a number of dollars.

"Too deep for me, boss," he admitted sadly. "Come on, be a good sport an' slip us th' info."

"Surely, James," and Mr. Clackworthy laughed, "there is nothing necessarily peculiar about my treating my able assis-tants to a vacation in the country. You and I have a place a little farther down the street; it will be a nice, quiet spot for my reading — when I am not busy looking after the factory; none of the squawking automobile horns that distract those who dwell along Sheridan Road."

The remark about the quiet spot for reading was adding fuel to The Early Bird's already flaming indignation, for he detested his idol's habit of browsing leisurely through his clas-sical volumes. "Factory!" exploded The Early Bird. "What's a factory gotta do with liftin' a bunch of coin off'n these gamblin' fellers? Moreover I ain't gonna be stuck off in the woods like this."

"What if I should have been thoughtful enough to defy that particular section of the Volstead Act which relates to the transportation of liquors from place to place?" asked Mr. Clackworthy.

"Well, if you brought along enough of the redeye," amended The Early Bird, "mebbe I can manage t' drown my sorrow. But it's sure gonna help me bear up under the burden if I'm let in on the know."

"Oh, we won't get lonesome. There'll be quite a colony of us. There's 'Pop' Blanchard."

"You've rung Pop in on it?"

"Yes, James; he's to be manager of the factory."

"Some elaborate layout!" exclaimed The Early Bird. "You must be figgurin' on cleanin' up quite a pile of the yellow stuff.

What kinda factory is this, anyhow?"

"A mattress factory," replied Mr. Clackworthy, "I found a concern in Chicago that was in financial straits. At the same time I was fortunate enough to find a jobbing house that needed five thousand mattresses. Until this order is filled, at any rate, Wardsville's new industry, housed in the long-deserted factory building here, will make expenses. Any profits we make from — er — other sources will be clear,"

"Yeah," commented The Early Bird, "it oughta be pretty soft, the mattress business."

III.

Within a week the ten residents of Wardsville, the little handful left of the three hundred souls when the town gave promise of amounting to something, were dazed to find a thriving industry operating in their midst. The population was swelled to about fifty, which included Mr. Clackworthy and his immediate fellow conspirators, as well as the thirty-odd mattress makers who had been imported from the city.

It was somewhat reminiscent of the days when Wardsville had been founded. The workers in the new factory got free rent of their cottages, and their groceries and household supplies were sold to them at cost by the small cooperative store which Mr. Clackworthy had established. Some inducement, it was true, had been needed to get the men away from the city.

Ten years before, Philo Ward had founded the town. He built his manufacturing plant on the theory that the employees should share in the profits. The test remained unproven, for, shortly after it was started, Philo Ward died, and those who inherited his money did not inherit his ideas. They scouted the profit-sharing business as a silly piece of foolishness and put a stop to it. Wardsville's houses were emptied, the factory closed, and Philo Ward's home, on the edge of the newly founded town, boarded up. It was an elaborate place, fitted out in elaborate, but erratic style; the heirs, who lived in Europe, had not even bothered to move out the furnishings and paintings. The entire property was put in the hands of an agent, but no one wanted to buy.

This was the situation when certain gentlemen in Chicago, sizing up things, had seen a great opportunity. They leased the Ward home and established in it their roulette wheels and poker tables where, not infrequently, it was said, a thousand dollars was won and lost on the turn of a card.

The Ward home was within the corporate limits of the village of Wardsville. And that was where Sam Clark came in. Sam Clark, after the exodus, kept his cottage and eked out an existence with his chickens and his truck garden. He was postmaster because no one else wanted the job; he became mayor for the same reason. It was no difficulty to get himself, in addition, appointed a police officer. He was one of those fellows who liked to look over the documents, signed by the governor and the president, certifying his offices.

Being of a naturally curious bent, Sam Clark nosed around a bit when the old Ward home was reopened and autoists began to travel the narrow road which led to the place. His curiosity was well rewarded. Mr. Ambrose Castleman, who conducted the outlawed pastime at the Ward place, had a heart-to-heart talk with Sam Clark, with the result that Sam Clark quit gardening and gathering eggs but, despite his apparent shiftlessness, began to roll in money.

Truth to tell, Sam Clark got a hundred and fifty dollars a week for failing to invoke the duties of his office.

Castleman's gambling house was frequented by a very high-class clientele, for Ambrose Castleman knew that the "squawks" generally came from losers who could not afford to lose. Therefore he saw to it that those who played at his gaming tables were those who would never miss the money; or, if they did miss it, to keep their grief to themselves. No strangers were admitted.

The days sped past, and still Mr. Clackworthy failed to enlighten his puzzled coworkers as to the details of his plot. The Early Bird, Mr. and Mrs. Bascom, and Pop Blanchard held frequent guessing contests, but, even by their combined stretches of imagination, they could not hypothesize any connection between a mattress factory and the Castleman gambling house.

Mr. Castleman himself, sleek, soft-voiced, and crafty, viewed the new population with a vague annoyance. Wardsville, because of its isolation and lack of folk who might show a disposition to pry into his peculiar and profitable business, made it an ideal location; and the success of his establishment was predicated on the assumption that its seclusion insured complete privacy.

However, as the days passed and none of the new residents showed any concern regarding anything except the mattress factory, Mr. Castleman turned his mind to other matters and probably would have dismissed it entirely, except that he received a visit from Mr. Amos Clackworthy. It happened that Mr. Clackworthy chose a time of day when Mr. Castleman was in an impatient frame of mind.

It was early in the morning — ten o'clock, to be exact — and, as most of the gaming was done at night, this was about Mr. Castleman's retiring hour. He was quite tired and very sleepy. He looked up impatiently as he received the man whom he knew to be the head of the town's new industry.

"Yes, yes, Mr. — er — Clackworthy," he said, glancing at the card, "what can I do for you?"

"I am very grateful to you, Mr. Castleman, for this interview," said the confidence man genially, "and I am quite sure that you, in time, will be grateful to me. You have doubtless heard something of the new industry which I have established in Wardsville?"

"Yes," assented Castleman in a colorless voice.

"I had best begin by saying," pursued Mr. Clackworthy, "that I have long admired the industrial theory propounded and advocated by the late Philo Ward. However, I think he carried it too far — much too far. But more of that in a moment, I am here to explain to you that the Wardsville Mattress Company is but the nucleus to be operated on a modified theory such as outlined by Mr. Ward himself."

"What has that to do with me?" demanded Castleman with a show of asperity.

"Just a moment, my dear Mr. Castleman," genially continued Mr. Clackworthy. "Please have patience. As you, of course, do not need to be told, a manufacturing concern gets its maximum production with contented workmen. And that is the late Mr. Ward's theory — contented labor. We have now been operating the Wardsville Mattress Company some weeks; every one of our employees is a satisfied employee. We are paying a higher wage than for the same work in the city; we are getting more production. Now to get down to brass tacks:

"I have taken a lease and option on the factory building and all of the store buildings and cottages of the Ward estate — except this house which you occupy. My plan is to enlarge the mattress factory, to fill the remaining vacant cottages; then to launch other factories — canning factories, broom factories, clothing factories, shirt factories, hat factories, lace factories."

"You're taking in a large territory," Mr. Castleman said with a sneer. "I repeat, how does this interest me?"

"We are going to crawl before we start walking," replied Mr. Clackworthy. "Each industry will stand on its own merits. In a few years houses will stretch over this country as far as the eye can see. The capital stock of our present company —"

"I see," snorted Mr. Castleman, "a stock-selling scheme. You're wasting your time — and mine, which is more important."

"Just a moment," protested Mr. Clackworthy insistently. "The present capital stock of our company is small — only seventy thousand dollars. We propose to make this the parent company, and all who subscribe for stock in the parent company will receive, as a bonus, share for share in all of the succeeding companies. I understand that you are a man of means, and —"

"Aw, you make me sick!" exploded Mr. Castleman with abrupt frankness. "Get out of here with your visionary schemes. I want to go to bed; get out."

Mr. Clackworthy smiled pleasantly.

"Mr. Castleman," he said chuckling, "I'm willing to lay you a little bet; I'll bet you five hundred dollars, two to one, that you will see the advantages of owning this stock before the end of thirty days."

Castleman glanced up quickly.

"I'm a sportsman; I don't deal in sure things," he refused.

IV.

Sam Clark — pardon us, Mayor Clark — was sitting on

the porch of his little office proudly gazing upon a pair of dia-
mond-studded cuff links which he had only the day before purchased in the city. Diamonds were his mania. Glancing up
dreamily, he frowned.

Across the street he saw The Early Bird, tack hammer in
hand, nailing up some sort of printed notice.

"Hey!" he called. "Whatcha doin'?"

"Whatcha think I'm doin'?" retorted The Early Bird with
utter lack of respect for the mayoral dignity.

Red of face at the rebuff, Mayor Clark got to his feet and
ambled over to where he could read the printed matter. The
top line, in heavy black type, announced: "Mass meeting
tonight."

This in itself was startling, for in years there had been no
gathering of the local citizenry.

"Mass meeting!" exclaimed Mayor Clark. "I ain't heard
nothin' about no mass meetin'."

"Well, you're hearin' about it now," retorted The Early
Bird. "That's what I'm tackin' up these here bills for. Better
come out; liable t'got an earful."

Mayor Clark found the notice briefly disconcerting, it continued:

WHEREAS a municipal election is to be held in the town of
Wardsville on the fourth day of next month, for the election of a
mayor and other municipal officers; and

WHEREAS the town of Wardsville is much in need of
sweeping reforms for its civic betterment, a mass meeting has
been called for tonight at the factory of the Wardsville Mattress
Company to discuss candidates.

Mayor Clark gulped and blinked and made a queer,
squeaky noise in his throat.

"W-who had them notices printed?" he demanded when
he could find his voice.

The Early Bird drew himself up sternly.

"Read the signature — an' weep!" he declared grandly.
"There it is at the bottom of the bill — The Wardsville Civic
Improvement Association, Mr. Amos Clackworthy, chair-
man."

"B-but," Mayor Clark spluttered, "I — I have been mayor for five years, an' —" He stopped in sudden panic as he realized that the ten voters who had stood by him so loyally during the past five years would not be the only ones to go to the polls now.

"Where — where will I find Mr. — Mr. Clackworthy?" he asked. "I — I would like to have a talk with him."

"Gone t' the big city, but I reckon he'll be back in time t' deliver a stirrin' address before the mass meetin'," replied The Early Bird maliciously, as he strode off down the street to continue his temporary job as billposter.

That evening the office of the Wardsville mattress factory was filled; which is to say that some twenty of the employees were attending the mass meeting by personal request. Early in the proceedings Mayor Clark slipped inside and hung uncertainly at the rear, hoping for the best and fearing for the worst. He didn't like the cool, businesslike way that Mr. Amos Clackworthy, presiding at the table, opened the meeting. Rapping for order, Mr. Clackworthy got to his feet and fixed the little gathering with a steady gaze which rested for several accusing seconds on Mayor Clark.

"Gentlemen," he began, "we are about to form the permanent organization of the Wardsville Civic Improvement Association. Our town is face to face with a glorious future We are soon to expand, to grow, and to prosper. In this future civic progress we must turn our eye toward civic betterment, to see that municipal officers of the highest possible caliber are elected; men who will lend their efforts and their influence to the best civic interests. Perhaps all of you are not aware that a very shameful condition now exists within our town's limits — gambling for high stakes!"

Mayor Clark winced; what he had feared was happening.

"Mind you," continued Mr. Clackworthy, "I do not accuse the present officials of abetting this immoral condition for any personal gain, but the fact that such a condition does exist, means that our present officials are inefficient, at least. This condition must be stopped, and, since those now in power have not stopped it, we must elect to office at the forthcoming election men who will. The question before the meeting tonight is — who will be those men? Who will we elect for mayor?"

"You! You!" shouted The Early Bird, George Bascom, and Pop Blanchard in unison. "You!" echoed the faithful employees of the Wardsville Mattress Company.

"My friends," said Mr. Clackworthy with feeling, "I greatly appreciate this spontaneous tribute to your faith in me. In the face of such a storm of public approval I would be derelict in my duty as a citizen did I not offer my humble efforts to carry out the will of the better element of our fair community. I shall be most happy to announce my candidacy for mayor, and I promise you that if I am elected I shall stamp out this flagrant evil to which I have previously referred."

"Some spellbinder!" chuckled The Early Bird proudly.

"If I am elected," pursued Mr. Clackworthy with a smile, "I announce now that I shall name to the office of town marshal a man who will enforce the law as befits an appreciation of the solemn oath of office — Mr. James Early. I shall have Mr. Early address you with a few words in which he will assure you that he will not fail in his duty."

The Early Bird was considerably flustered at being called upon to make a public speech, for Mr. Clackworthy, with a joke up his sleeve, had not warned him that he would be called upon. But The Early Bird was game. He got to his feet and, after opening and closing his mouth several times without being able to get any words to roll forth, forced the first halting sounds through his lips.

"The boss here — I mean Mr. Clackworthy — has slipped you the right dope, I'm tellin' the world that while I ain't never been a flatfoot, I'm hep to the game." And he winked at Mr. Clackworthy, which was to say that what he referred to was the days when one of his chief occupations was dodging the police. "I'm puttin' my O. K. on the boss' remarks that when he is mayor of this burg, an' I'm wearin' the nickel-plated star an' jinglin' a pair of come-alongs in my pocket, there ain't gonna be no guys pilin' up a stack of the yellow stuff with no loaded dice or marked cards. I'm a little lame on performin' with the English langwidge, an' the old chin don't wag free an' easy when it comes t' the big words like it does t' some, but if the boss, here, puts me in as chief of police an' tells me t' run the gamblers outta town — well, the minute the ballots is counted an' they see that the boss wins in the final score, they'd better be huntin' a fresh place t' hang their hats; for I'll be on the job."

The Early Bird, perspiring with his oratorical effort, slumped down in his chair, as Mr. Clackworthy, laughing silently, clapped vigorously.

Mayor Sam Clark, who had come to the meeting with the intention of speaking a little piece himself, decided that it was no place for him and slunk miserably out of the hall. As fast as his almost trembling legs would carry him he hurried to the old Ward home to carry the sad tidings that the town had been struck by a small but devastating tornado of reform.

V.

"Boss," said The Early Bird when he and Mr. Clackworthy had returned to their own modest Wardsville cottage after the mass meeting, "I'm just beginnin' t' get this here game through the old bean. I gotcha!"

"Do you, indeed, James?"

"Sure! You're gonna get yourself elected mayor, an' I'm gonna pull a raid on this here swell gamblin' emporium an' make that Castleman goof talk turkey. We're gonna shake 'em down for a few bales of centuries."

Mr. Clackworthy lifted his palms in righteous horror.

"James!" he exclaimed. "You are intimating that I would corrupt a public office by accepting a bribe. Do I look like a man who would prostitute my public trust? No, James, I promise you that if I am elected mayor I shall carry out my platform and stamp out gambling."

"Then what's the lay?" pleaded The Early Bird. "Of course you're gonna be elected; with all the help at the factory votin' for you, you gotta win!"

"I think you are about to learn the answer," replied Mr. Clackworthy as a motor stopped out in front of the cottage. "My guess, James, is that Mr. Castleman is calling on us. Listen to me very closely, for I am going to let you entertain Mr. Castleman for a few minutes while I step outside."

Mr. Clackworthy spoke hurriedly but in terse, enlightening sentences that caused The Early Bird to nod quickly.

When Mr. Castleman entered the living room he found The Early Bird alone.

"Where'll I find this Clackworthy fellow?" demanded Castleman.

"Have a chair," invited James. "He'll be back in a coupla shakes."

Mr. Castleman ignored the invitation, contenting himself with striding angrily up and down the room. He was discouraged by the appearance of the room; certainly this was not the abode of some fly-by-night promoter; the furnishings bespoke a solidity of character, a man of culture.

"Humph!" he grunted. "Kind of a queer fellow, this Clackworthy, eh?"

"You've said it!" exclaimed The Early Bird. "He's a nut!" If there was any friendship between him and Mr. Clackworthy, James' voice failed to reveal it; in fact one would have guessed just the opposite.

"The very idear of him wastin' his time on this reform foolishness," continued The Early Bird bitterly. "He's got his hands full as it is. Gonna make me chief of police! Of course I had t' agree with him — with all the dough I got tied up in this here factory business."

Mr. Castleman glanced up quickly.

"Then I take it," he said, "that you are not in sympathy with this — er — meeting tonight."

"I'm in sympathy with it just like the owner of a brewery is in sympathy with Volstead for president," retorted The Early Bird. "I like t' draw five cards m'self. But what's a guy gonna do? This Clackworthy bozo's got all my coin, an' I'm tryin' to jar him loose from it. I'm gettin' kinda shaky about this here village turnin' out t' be a second Chicago."

"I think you would be!" scoffingly stated Mr. Castleman. "Well, there's one consolation; the bubble will burst pretty soon."

"An' that's just where you're wrong," argued The Early Bird. "The way things is runnin' now, the factory's breakin' even. It's when he goes t' spreadin' out that fish is gonna be hooked. An' Mr. Clackworthy's got dough, too; we'll last a coupla years, believe me."

"He will!" groaned Mr. Castleman. "A couple of years!"

The reason for his grief was that only a few days before he had been so sure of his possession of a good thing, that he had purchased the Ward property outright. But that was more or less a minor consideration; his profits were enormous. "Isn't there some way to stop him?"

"Not a chance."

"I thought," said Mr. Castleman shrewdly, "that if I became — er — associated with this Mr. Clackworthy in a — umph — a business way, won his friendship by investing in his company, that perhaps he might — er — forget this reform business of his."

"Not a chance," grunted The Early Bird.

Mr. Castleman exploded with some blistering words.

The Early Bird assumed a pose of deep thought.

"I gotta hunch," he said slowly. "How much would it be worth t' you t' get Mr. Clackworthy outta this burg?"

"That depends," answered Mr. Castleman evasively.

"Then lemme spill a few words in your ear," said The Early Bird, and briefly he whispered his plan. Hardly had he finished when the door opened, and Mr. Clackworthy came in.

"Ah, good evening, Mr. Castleman," he said pleasantly. "This visit is more or less a surprise to me." Which was quite truthful, for it was much less a surprise than Mr. Castleman imagined.

"I called to talk about your promotion scheme," began Mr. Castleman, manufacturing a fair imitation of cordiality. "Since thinking things over and noting your — er — progress, I thought I might invest, after all; in fact, make a substantial investment."

"Just a minute, Mr. Castleman," interrupted Mr. Clackworthy. "Without malice I wish to inform you that your becoming a stockholder will not at all change my attitude toward your — er — unlawful occupation. Pardon me if I accuse you of ulterior motives; if you wish to come in as a bona fide investor, I welcome you; but if you are trying to divert me from a principle you are wasting your time."

"This is purely an investment with me," replied Mr. Castleman. "That being settled, let's get down to business. Your company is incorporated for fifty thousand dollars. I will buy half of your stock."

"You surprise me!" exclaimed Mr. Clackworthy. "So large an investment! But I could not part with control, you know. I will sell you no more than twenty-two thousand dollars' worth of the stock — not a penny more. I would not even sell you that much, except that it will enable me to rush my plans to a more speedy consummation."

"Done!" said Mr. Castleman promptly. He knew when to play a pat hand.

It may seem surprising that the gambling-house owner should have agreed so willingly to part with such a large sum of money, but he knew that he could resell a large part of it to his patrons, mostly rich men, who would be willing to reimburse him for the privilege of continuing their quiet games in his establishment. He could think of a dozen who would take a thousand dollars' worth each.

"If you have the certificates, sign them over right now, and I'll give you my check," continued Mr. Castleman.

"It happens that I do have them," nodded Mr. Clackworthy.

And it was but the matter of a moment to complete the transaction. Before surrendering his check, however, Mr. Castleman turned to The Early Bird.

"And, now," he said, "I will buy your stock, Mr. Early. Turn over your shares. You see, Clackworthy," he went on triumphantly, "I do control your company, after all; with the shares that I get from Early, here, I own the majority of stock. I shall take over the affairs of the company tomorrow and have myself elected president."

"I — I don't understand," said Mr. Clackworthy, with well-simulated confusion. "Why — what do you propose to do?"

"That will be decided later, when I am in charge," replied Mr. Castleman sharply, and, gathering up his stock certificates, he jammed his hat on his head and strode out of the house.

When the gambling-house owner had gone, Mr. Clackworthy laughed with unrestrained mirth.

"He thinks that he has pulled a master stroke," he said.

"Yeah," said The Early Bird, grinning. "He thinks he's puttin' one over on us. Tomorrow he'll close down the factory, an' all the employees'll have t' move back t' the city to get other jobs. Then the ten goofs what's been votin' for Sam Clark for five years will vote for him again — say, that's rich! Boss, I'll say you're opposed t' gamblin'; you always play the sure shots."

"But I do gamble, James," retorted Mr. Clackworthy, still laughing, "and that's just where the joke does come in; I was gambling on Castleman being so badly scared by our little reform movement that he wouldn't look up the law. Why, James, I haven't been a resident of Wardsville long enough to qualify as mayor; the charter demands that the mayor shall have been a citizen of the town at least two years prior to his election!"

The Early Bird sighed.

"Boss," he said, "I know we cleaned up a few thou' on this scheme, an' we had a lotta fun doin' it, but just the same I sure would have liked t' be a chief of police — even of a hick town."

MR. CLACKWORTHY
SELLS SHORT

Just outside the entrance of the Grain Exchange, famous the world over as "The Pit," stood Mr. Clackworthy. What Wall Street is to the stock market, The Pit is to the grain market. It is here that seemingly frantic men — in reality cold, shrewd, calculating beneath their breathless haste — determine the price of the goods from nature's storehouse. The hurrying and scurrying, the lifting of a finger, a whispered conference in a secluded corner, and the price of a loaf of bread may advance a penny the following week.

"A guy 'ud think he'd wandered to th' nut house." commented The Early Bird, who stood by Mr. Clackworthy's side. "These ginks act like th' heat had turned their beans."

"Appearances are deceitful, James," said Mr. Clackworthy wisely; "unless you brand any sort of gambling as insanity, these men whom you see bartering in wheat, oats, corn, and other grains of the field, are most unusually alert mentally. Ah —"

The Early Bird glanced up quickly at the master confidence man's sudden pause and let his eyes follow the gaze of Mr. Clackworthy.

"Holy Hollywood!" cried James. "Is th' peepers seein' things, or is they stagin' a movie stunt with that layout?"

"Your vision is unimpaired, and it is not a cinema stunt," replied Mr. Clackworthy with a smile. "You see approaching you in that ancient equipage — a king."

"A king!" repeated The Early Bird scornfully. "Whatcha tryin' to do, kid me?"

Proceeding with majestic deliberation toward the Grain Exchange was a carriage drawn by two splendid horses. On the box were liveried coachman and footman. The carriage itself, while luxurious and sporting a glossy new coat of paint, was of ancient pattern — one of those ancient private coaches belonging to a period of more than a quarter of a century previous.

"Truly, a king," insisted Mr. Clackworthy; "the occupant of that carriage is none other than Ashton Scott, whose scepter rules the wheat market with as much tyranny as ever ruled a Nero."

"Aw, I gotcha," said The Early Bird, nodding; "you mean that's Ashton Scott, th' wheat king."

"So acclaimed by the grain world," agreed Mr. Clackworthy; "it is Ashton Scott who, by the price he puts on wheat, fixes the price of bread. It is due to the fact that he cornered the wheat market — and kept it cornered — that the long-suffering, helpless public is now paying ten cents a loaf — and gets smaller loaves.

"It is common gossip that he has made fifteen million dollars out of wheat through his corner; while, perhaps, he does not share the common odium of the term 'profiteer,' the appellation fits him, he is as ruthlessly a profiteer as any of them — a profiteer in wheat. Perhaps, James, you do not realize how other prices climb when wheat goes up; wheat is a general price barometer. And, thus it is, Ashton Scott is one of the worst profiteers of them all."

The Early Bird was paying but small attention to Mr. Clackworthy's economic dissertation; his eyes were fixed, with a puzzled expression, on the nearing carriage.

"Mother of Mud! That sure gets my goat," he said musingly. "What's a gink with all his coin want to go poking around in that outfit for? Why don't a bozo with all his jack turn them horses out to pasture and loosen up about five thousand seeds for a good buzz buggy? How's a guy as out o' date as that manage to keep his place in this kale-grabbin' contest?"

"His carriage may be only two-horsepower, James," and — Mr. Clackworthy laughed, "but there are dozens, yes, hundreds, of men here on The Pit that can assure you that his hat covers a ninety-horse-power brain. Take a look at him."

The carriage drew up at the curb; the footman descended and opened the door. Messenger boys suddenly ceased to be in a hurry — they stopped to stare. Traders halted in their steps with an awed look at the small man who stepped to the sidewalk; the hum of conversation died to a whisper; a motorman halted his trolley in the middle of the block that he might peer at the famous figure.

The Wheat King was about to mount his throne! This monarch had no cabinet of ministers; his royal decrees were handed down without the consultation of trusted advisers and often they shook the market like a bolt from a clear sky. No man could anticipate his plans or decisions; those who pretended to guess his probable action generally guessed wrong. He was Absolute Monarch of the wheat market; it was a one-man rule.

The Early Bird had heard much of him but had never seen the grain wizard before. He knew, of course, that Ashton Scott was an old man; but he had expected to see a virile viking, bristling with dynamic energy.

"Great Goshen!" exclaimed James. "What a runt! Is that th' guy that all these ginks is afraid of?"

Ashton Scott, an old-fashioned knitted scarf thrown about his thin and drooping shoulders, was less than five-feet-six. His face was thin and bloodless — but the eyes: they showed his power!

Gleaming from under a heavy pair of brows, they glared fearlessly from over a long, eagle nose; they seemed to scorch and sear everything they touched. Those eyes told of an iron will, of singular lack of the softer sentiments; men shriveled up and slunk away before their steady gaze.

Involuntarily, The Early Bird took a step backward.

"Lor!" he breathed; "what a pair of peepers that bozo's got!"

"A wonderful personality — provided that you do not use wonderful as a term of praise," commented Mr. Clackworthy. "A greedy misanthropist, is what he is."

Ashton Scott made his deliberate way up the steps of the Grain Exchange and to the offices where he held sway. Men he passed would have given a right arm to know the secrets which lay under that battered old hat.

Mr. Clackworthy stood for several minutes, meditatively eying the ancient carriage of Ashton Scott; his face lighted.

"James," he said softly, "I've got it — I've got it!"

"Whatcha got?" demanded The Early Bird.

"The scheme that will bring Ashton Scott's throne tumbling down about his ears — and line our pockets with many crisp yellow bills."

The Early Bird, still under the spell of the Wheat King's rapier-like gaze, shuddered and shook his head.

"Not for every dollar in th' U. S. treasury, down to th' last tail of th' last Buffalo nickel," he refused.

Mr. Clackworthy chuckled.

"Very well, James," he said easily, "suppose, then, that you stand on the side lines, so to speak, and see me take a little whirl at the stock market, for the name of Ashton Scott is Number Two of my list in our war on the profiteers."

"What's th' lay?" asked The Early Bird.

Mr. Clackworthy shook his head teasingly. Then he chuckled:

"You just watch, James."

II.

It was two days later and The Early Bird was pacing restlessly up and down the thick, imported rug of Mr. Clackworthy's Sheridan Road apartment, fairly eaten up by curiosity. Although the master confidence man had not stirred from the big, luxuriously furnished library except for two trips downtown, both of brief duration, he knew that Mr. Clackworthy had not surrendered his plot on the riches of Ashton Scott and returned to his cherished classics.

He was hoping that Mr. Clackworthy might relent and take him into his confidence concerning the ways and means planned to dethrone the Wheat King, yet he hesitated to ask. He decided on a bit of strategy, and tried to achieve an air of great indifference. He yawned and stretched his arms.

"Well, I see you an' the highbrows is chummin' together again," he said; "kinda reckon you've given up th' notion of puttin' th' stinger on th' Wheat King, eh? Kinda decided to let 'im wear his wheat-straw crown, eh?"

Mr. Clackworthy read behind these questions and smiled.

"Oh, by no means, James," he denied; "the little scheme is coming along very well, indeed. I put up an even twenty-five thousand in margins on wheat futures today; I'm taking my little whirl at the market — first time I have ever ventured, too."

The Early Bird stared in frank perplexity.

"Say, whatcha givin' me?" he demanded. "You put up twenty-five thousand in margins — and expect that to give Ashton Scott a trimmin'? Huh! That's like one of them lake excursion boats givin' battle to th' Atlantic Fleet. Twenty-five thousand! Now, ain't that rich — and old Scott worth right around that many million! Whatcha tryin' to do, furnish me with a laugh?"

Mr. Clackworthy grinned.

"It won't work, James," he said.

"O' course 'twon't work," retorted The Early Bird triumphantly.

"What I meant that would not work," explained Mr. Clackworthy, "was your obvious effort to catch me off my guard and take you into my confidence. I haven't kept you in suspense for some time, James; I'm going to have to whet your curiosity a bit."

The Early Bird smiled sheepishly that his subterfuge had been so easily penetrated.

"You win th' leather medal for th' mind-readin' contest," he admitted; "come on, boss, let me see th' wheels go 'round."

"Well, James, I'll throw a little hint or so — and see how good a guesser you are.

"Naturally I am not simple-minded enough to imagine that a meager little twenty-five thousand dollars is going to prove sufficient ammunition to accomplish the defeat of Ashton Scott and break his wheat corner; that, of course, is absurd. The twenty-five thousand, truth to tell, has nothing to do with the actual war on the Wheat King; that is a mere incident which allows me to collect a fee for accomplishing the public benefaction of breaking Scott's grip on the grain market.

"The real plan of strategy — well, that's the dark and mysterious secret which is so puzzling you, James."

"Give a guy a chance, boss," pleaded The Early Bird; "slip me a little info' — gimme a hint of what's comin' off."

Mr. Clackworthy smoked quietly for a moment.

"I took a little stroll down to The Pit this morning, James; I found the traders very nervous and jumpy; and it's all on account of Ashton Scott's birthday.

"For a good many years now his birthday has always been

marked by a big flurry in grain futures. At first it was thought to be mere coincidence, but it is now reasonably certain that it's a little practical joke of Scott's. Being the strongest and the most merciless man in The Pit, he is naturally the most hated; it seems to be an ironical bit of humor of his to force his enemies — they are all his enemies mostly down there — to give him a substantial birthday present every year.

"Anyway, every year on Ashton Scott's birthday there are big doings in The Pit. Sometimes the prices break; at other times they skyrocket to dizzy heights — and once in a while they do both, with old Scott collecting on a double manipulation. The result is that the traders are keeping one eye on the calendar and the other on their bank balance — and praying that they will be lucky enough to jump with Ashton Scott.

"There is a rather terrifying rumor being whispered about that something bigger than ever is to happen this year; that the Wheat King is about to pull his greatest coup, accept his largest compulsory birthday present and retire to his lonely existence in his gloomy old house on Dearborn Street — a mansion as old fashioned as the carriage which you saw carry the old highwayman downtown the other day."

"And," ventured The Early Bird with a bit of sarcasm, "I guess you've trotted out th' old Ouija board, and that Ouija has given you th' plumb low-down on just how Scott's gonna work th' game; an' you're gonna tip off all his enemies so's they can be layin' for 'im with a piece of gas pipe and spoil his pretty little birthday party — an' you're gonna ride into harbor with a coupla hundred thousand in your kick."

"Please do not be silly, James," said Mr. Clackworthy reprovingly. "Besides your metaphors are hopelessly mixed. Mull it over in your mind for a day or so; I think that I shall let you in on it in time to be on the stage when the curtain rises on the big act.

"One thing I will tell you: I have no more idea than you have what Ashton Scott proposes to do — and what he proposes to do is really a matter of indifference to me for — well, he won't do it!"

III.

When Mr. Clackworthy took the wheel of his big touring car, set his foot on the starter button and drove southward, he was unaware that The Early Bird, determined to get some inkling of the mystery, had slipped out of the Sheridan Road apartment behind him, got into a taxicab after giving the chauffeur instructions to follow.

The little task of harmless shadowing took The Early Bird to a number of queer places. Mr. Clackworthy drove somewhat leisurely to Diversey Parkway, and westward over to Clark Street. At a garage where a sign announced:

USED AUTOMOBILES FOR SALE.

Mr. Clackworthy stopped and got out. The Early Bird drew the curtains of the taxi which permitted him to have the chauffeur draw up at the curb without fear that Mr. Clackworthy would uncover his bit of curiosity-satisfying detective work. He saw the master confidence man negotiating with the owner of the establishment, and finally close some sort of a transaction; from the number of bills which changed hands, The Early Bird felt morally certain that Mr. Clackworthy had purchased a secondhand automobile.

"Now, what'n th' name of all that's holy does th' boss want with a secondhand buzz buggy?" he ruminated. "I'll say he's a deep un."

Mr. Clackworthy returned to his own car and continued his way southward on Clark Street for a few blocks. At Belden Avenue he drove west a short distance and turned into an alleyway.

"I wonder if he's got wise to th' fact that I'm trailin' him an' is tryin' to make a monkey outta me," muttered The Early Bird. He had the taxicab pause at the mouth of the alley and gave the chauffeur an extra dollar to pretend to be jimmying with the motor. From this vantage point, James was able to see his mentor proceed between the double row of dilapidated, tumble-down sheds and come to a halt before one of them.

"Now, when Mr. Clackworthy takes to comin's down alleys, I give up," stuttered The Early Bird in amazement. Carefully marking in his mind the location of the shed at which the master confidence man had stopped, he had the chauffeur proceed around the corner to the other end of the passageway from which Mr. Clackworthy would naturally emerge. But, whether intentional or not, Mr. Clackworthy did the unexpected; he turned his car around and made his exit at the same end by which he had entered.

After waiting for half an hour or more, The Early Bird took a peek up the alley; it was empty. Mr. Clackworthy had, accidentally or otherwise, evaded him.

"Dog-gone his buttons," The Early Bird grumbled, "I was gonna get a line on this scheme of his if I had to follow him all day — and now he's gone! Secondhand gas buggies; visits up alleys and — some kind scheme to put th' stinger on old Ashton Scott! Honest, now, wouldn't that make Solomon wrinkle a puzzled brow; I'm askin' you, wouldn't it?"

Dismissing the taxi, James decided to learn, if he could, what key to the mystery was contained in that shed which Mr. Clackworthy had just visited. He made his way up the dirt-clogged passageway until he reached the tumbledown place in question.

From the other side of the thin wooden door, he heard a vaguely familiar voice singing, in subdued bass, the strains of an old-fashioned air. The Early Bird rapped. The singing stopped, there was the crunching of shoes over the floor, and a bright eye gleamed through a knot hole in one of the boards.

"Well?" demanded the deep voice. "Oh, it's The Early Bird; wait till I open the door."

The rusty hinges creaked and James was admitted into the shed, a cobwebby place measuring some fifteen feet square.

"Why, hello, Wally," greeted The Early Bird; the man was Waldo Gleason, one of the boys whom Mr. Clackworthy occasionally relied upon to perform a task incident with one of his schemes. Waldo was not very talented, but he was close-mouthed; that meant something.

"Lookin' for Mr. Clackworthy, eh?" suggested Wally. "He just left."

"Yeah; I know," replied The Early Bird; "I seen him. Say, Wally, what th' devil is that thing and whatcha doing to it?"

"Well," answered Wally with a twinkle in his eye,

"judging from what I've seen of such, I'd say that thing mounted on those four wheels and ornamented with a big brass gong on the dashboard is what is commonly known and denominated as — an ambulance. As for the second half of your question, I am painting it."

"Whatcha paintin' it for?"

"For the good and sufficient reason that one Mr. Amos Clackworthy has given me a hundred dollars to paint it."

"What's he want it painted for?"

"Now, you've got me there, old socks; I didn't ask any questions. I reckoned that if Mr. Clackworthy wanted me to know the whys and wherefores, he would have out with it. But don't you know; you and him are as thick as molasses in January."

"This is one he ain't let me in on," replied The Early Bird with a sigh; "he's got a hen on, but he wants me to guess what it is. I leave it to you now, a guy couldn't guess in a thousand guesses what an ambulance would have to do annexin' a few thousand shekels of some bird's dough."

"And I'm not going to try to guess; I've a headache," said Wally.

"Well, I'm beginnin' to get a pain in th' old bean, too," said The Early Bird, "but mine comes from doin' too much guessin'."

IV.

"James," said Mr. Clackworthy, "tomorrow is the day."

"Whatcha mean, th' day?"

"Tomorrow is the anniversary of Ashton Scott's birth."

The Early Bird shot a quick glance at the ornate desk calendar which stood on Mr. Clackworthy's rosewood table and his face paled.

"You — you mean tomorrow's th' day when you're due to put th' bee on his nibs, th' Wheat King?" he queried amazedly.

"I do."

"Then, you're ruined!" cried James. "You can't get away from th' hoodoo — tomorrow's th' thirteenth!"

Mr. Clackworthy laughed scornfully at the superstitious notion.

"Even granting, James, that there was something in the ancient fear of the figure thirteen, the hoodoo has got to make a choice. It's either Mr. Scott or myself who is slated to enjoy some extremely bad luck — which brings it right back to ordinary. The hoodoo can't very well give his curse to both of us."

"Well, mebbe there's something in that line of chatter," admitted The Early Bird, wiping the perspiration from his brow with a gesture of much relief, "but you sure had me scared for a minute."

"I don't think we have anything to fear from a hoodoo," and Mr. Clackworthy smiled; "the thing that worries me more than anything is your ability to drive a car with such dexterity that you can smash a couple of wheels off of another vehicle without breaking your fool neck."

"W-what's that?" cried The Early Bird. "Say, whatcha handin' me?"

"I mean, James, that you are now invited to accept a commission in General Clackworthy's army, which is due to enter into a serious engagement at eight-thirty o'clock tomorrow morning; it will be called The Battle of Profiteers' Hill."

"Aw, tie a can to that kinda chin music," protested The Early Bird; "what I wanna know is what was that stuff you was spillin' about me ram-min' th' wheels of an auto into another gas cart. That don't listen good to yours truly."

"It's not another motor that you're to have a collision with, James, but a stately horse-drawn vehicle which —"

"I gotcha; I gotcha," interrupted The Early Bird, his eyes widening with sudden understanding. "You got it all framed up for me to step on th' gas and zip right into old Ashton Scott's Civil War bus, an' put th' old pirate outta business so he can't be on hand to pull off th' annual birthday party."

"James, you begin to show signs of real intelligence."

"But I might kill th' old boy!" objected James. "I won't do it."

"You must use discretion, of course," answered Mr. Clackworthy with a laugh; "you must hit the carriage hard enough — but not too hard."

"Yeah!" snorted The Early Bird sarcastically; "I gotta kill 'im dead, but not too dead. That's a nice easy order you're givin' me. If I don't knock him out so his old noddle quits workin', th' scheme's no good; if I hit 'im too hard, I can hear th' jury sayin': 'We find James Early guilty of murder in th' first degree.' Yeah; a fine, clever idea that you've thought up — nit!

"An' I guess that ambulance you got cached away over here off'n Belden Avenue is gonna dash up real handy an' you're gonna load Scott into it and cart him off somewheres to keep 'im from comin' to real sudden an' spillin' th' beans, eh?"

Mr. Clackworthy was genuinely surprised.

"You sly old dog!" he exclaimed with a chuckle. "How did you find out about that ambulance?"

"Aw, I ain't solid ivory, I reckon," replied The Early Bird evasively; "a guy's got ways of findin' out things, y'know. I ain't so much ivory that I'm gonna risk bumpin' off a millionaire wheat king — not even if I knowed he was gonna raise th' price of bread to two berries a loaf. Let 'im profiteer and be hanged to 'im. I like to hear th' rattle of good old iron men down in th' old kick, but I don't like it well enough to run th' risk of hearin' th' rattle of a key in an iron door that's lockin' me in from now on."

"James," assured Mr. Clackworthy, "this scheme has yet other ramifications that you know not of. You have known me for a long time; you know that I have never lied to you or misled you in any fashion. I've got a bit of a surprise at the end, but take my word for it, you are in no more danger of causing the death of Ashton Scott than you are of marrying a crown princess. Is that good enough for you?"

"Yeah; that's good enough for me," agreed The Early Bird.

V.

The Pit, not usually awakened into another day's life until well along toward nine o'clock, was swarming with tense-nerved, tight-lipped traders, long before eight. Many of them had slept but little; a few of them had not slept at all.

This was the day — Ashton Scott's birthday! The air vibrated with excitement and a cloud of uneasiness hung low over the Grain Exchange. What was Ashton Scott going to do? That was the question on every tongue.

As the hour of eight neared, an automobile of nondescript

appearance and doubtful age made its cylinder-missing way along the street and parked a block from the Grain Exchange. Even his closest friends would have experienced difficulty in recognizing the goggled, ulstered driver as the man who had been christened James Early and upon whom the police, in days gone by, had saddled the nickname of "The Early Bird."

James shared something of the nervousness which permeated the district. Despite the fact that he had Mr. Clackworthy's assurance that the plan was safe, he failed to like the looks of it; deliberately driving an automobile into a millionaire's carriage is a serious business.

At eight o'clock and thirty-five minutes the grain traders experienced a shock which multiplied their fears.

For years Ashton Scott's habits had moved with the clock hands; he arose at a certain hour, he breakfasted just so many minutes later; he retired at a certain time. He had an unaltering schedule, reduced, almost, to split seconds. When the wheat king's carriage drew up in front of The Pit there was no need to glance up at the big clock which ornamented the tower of the building across the street — it was bound to be nine o'clock.

The grain merchants and brokers, at eight-thirty-five, glanced up to see the famous, horse-drawn carriage majestically approaching.

"My watch must be wrong," muttered one of them, turning the hands up twenty-five minutes.

"Mine, too," chimed in another.

"Boys," declared a third, "somethin's a-popping! Your watches are right — look at the tower clock. Ashton Scott is getting down ahead of time! It must be something big to make old Scott break his routine; boys, I'm telling you, the devil's going to break loose in The Pit this morning."

Slowly the carriage approached.

The tubercular, asthmatic automobile had disappeared. The Early Bird, following instructions, had thrown in the clutch as the Scott carriage appeared some distance away; he circled the block and returned by the way of the stubby little street which ended almost directly in front of The Pit.

He throttled down the engine, driving at a snail's pace in order to give the Scott carriage time to reach the street intersection. He was not more than two hundred feet away when the horse-drawn vehicle appeared from behind the buildings.

The Early Bird's hands nearly fell from the steering wheel; seated on the box of the Scott carriage, erect and solemn in his blue livery and brass buttons, sat no other person than George Bascom; good, faithful old George upon whom Mr. Clackworthy could always rely.

This moment of hesitation almost wrecked The Early Bird's minute calculations; but he quickly recovered from his surprise and gave the palsied secondhand car the gas.

Fearfully, apprehensively the grain men, knowing that the man in the carriage would send them home richer or poorer, watched the approach of the vehicle. Suddenly a gasp went through the crowd.

From the short cross street shot out an automobile, zigzagging wildly as if the driver had lost control of the car; but it was headed toward Ashton Scott's carriage. The coachman was seen to lift his whip over the backs of the horses and the team leaped forward — but not in time.

The automobile, despite a wide swerve and a greatly slackened speed as the brake bands whined in smoking protest, crashed into the rear wheels of the Wheat King's carriage. The sound of splintering wood echoed along the street and the stately equipage collapsed as if the hand of a giant had crushed it.

"Mother of Mud!" gasped The Early Bird in horror. "I didn't know I was gonna hit 'im that hard; I'll bet my bank roll against a plugged nickel that I've killed th' old geezer."

But, remembering his instructions, James threw himself forward over the steering wheel and feigned unconsciousness. It took no acting to simulate the chalk-white, deathlike pallor; his face was bloodless with fear.

VI.

There were, perhaps, a hundred grain men who witnessed the crash; they stood for a moment in speechless horror before they raced to the spot where the wreckage littered the street.

George Bascom and Fred Little, the latter also employed

by Mr. Clackworthy, had leaped from the box to safety. They were tugging at the splintered, broken pieces of wood when the men of The Pit crowded around, many of them offering a helping hand.

"Is — is Ashton Scott dead?" was the whisper that went from mouth to mouth — and a hopeful light flickered in many an eye.

A tall man, wearing a professional-appearing Vandyke, a medical satchel in his hand, pushed his way through the curious throng which pressed about the debris. It was, of course, Mr. Clackworthy.

"Make way there," some one cried; "here's a doctor."

A moment later and enough of the wreckage was cleared away to reveal the inert form of a little, shrunken old man, a knitted shawl about his thin shoulders. His face was almost unrecognizable. As much as they hated him, the grain men shuddered.

Mr. Clackworthy knelt down beside the injured man, briskly but gently feeling for signs of breaks and prying open the eyelids for a professional look at the pupils. The victim stirred.

Mr. Clackworthy leaned closer.

"This man wants to speak to a fellow named Haddon," he said.

"Haddon? That's his office manager; I can get him in a jiffy," some one volunteered, and went racing off to Scott's office.

"Anybody know who this man is?" demanded Mr. Clackworthy.

The crowd laughed that any one should not know; they told him.

"Well, he's dying — sinking fast," said Mr. Clackworthy; he turned to George Bascom, who still stood near. "You are this man's servant, I take it; well, hop to the telephone and call an ambulance."

A moment later and Felix Haddon, coatless, hatless, and breathless, bored his way through the crowd.

"Is — is it true?" he gasped; he caught sight of the shawl-covered shoulders and the crimson-covered face. "Good heavens, it is!"

"Are you Mr. Haddon?" demanded Mr. Clackworthy. "This man — Scott, isn't it? — is dying; he has a message for you. I will see if he can talk now; he's sinking very fast, I fear."

Mr. Clackworthy leaned over the injured man.

"Here's Mr. Haddon, Mr. Scott," he said; "you have a message for him?"

He lowered his ear to the man's lips, which moved feebly.

"He says —"

"For Heaven's sake, man!" interrupted Haddon hoarsely; "don't shout it; don't tell all these wolves about it — whisper it! That message is for me — and for me alone!"

Mr. Clackworthy nodded understandingly, as he lowered his voice.

"He says," he whispered, but the sibilant carried to the first and even the second row of grain men who stood packed around, silent and wide-eyed, "he says — *sell!* Whatever that means."

But even the pseudo doctor did not know the vital significance of that magic word "sell," there were more than a hundred men within a child's stone throw who did know. The traders and brokers eyed each other eagerly; those who had not heard Mr. Clackworthy's stage whisper got the message from those who had. The crowd began to melt; men were dashing madly for their offices in the Grain Exchange, for in a moment, now, The Pit would open — and Ashton Scott said sell!

A policeman arrived at this juncture.

"Any one call an ambulance?" he demanded, and was told that this detail had not been overlooked. Almost coincident with the patrolman's arrival, the ambulance gong clanged and the big vehicle, with a red cross emblazoned on its side, clattered alongside.

Two men in the white duck suits of hospital interns leaped out with a stretcher and, under the direction of Mr. Clackworthy, placed the injured man on a stretcher.

In the excitement and awe over the fate of Ashton Scott, no one had seemed to notice The Early Bird, who sat slumped over the steering wheel of the automobile.

"Here's another man hurt," shouted George Bascom, pointing to James.

Mr. Clackworthy rushed over to The Early Bird examined him hurriedly and called the stretcher bearers.

"We'll have to take this chap along, too," he instructed briskly; "he's in a bad way."

Room was made for a second patient and The Early Bird loaded inside. One of the interns hopped to the front seat with the driver and the second, and Mr. Clackworthy leaped into the rear with the two patients. The gong clanged and the ambulance dashed off, leaving a slow-witted policeman and his notebook standing in the middle of the street, wondering just how he was to go about getting a satisfactory report of the accident.

VII.

The Early Bird, his eyes glued shut, heard a chuckle. Cautiously he partly opened one eye, which enabled him to observe Mr. Clackworthy in the act of lighting a cigar.

"Did — did I hurt 'im — bad?" whispered The Early Bird. "Gosh! I don't know how it happened; I was goin' slow and I didn't more'n touch that carriage but — bang — I musta hit it like a ton of bricks. He — he ain't gonna die, is he?"

"Is who going to die?" demanded Mr. Clackworthy.

"Ashton Scott, of course."

"Yes, I think he's going to die."

"An' you got me in this mess, an' you sit there grinnin'!" cried The Early Bird accusingly.

"Well, most people have to die some time, James," remarked Mr. Clackworthy dryly. "I won't worry you any longer, James; sit up and take a look. You are among friends, now."

The Early Bird blinked and stared through the gloom of the ambulance. The first thing he saw was Al Shipiro, immaculate in his white-duck uniform, calmly smoking a cigarette. The sight that next greeted his eyes was that of a thin man, a knitted shawl about his shoulders, rising to a sitting posture and begin mopping his face clean of the crimson stain which covered and obliterated his features. As the mask was wiped away, The Early Bird recognized the features of Chester Wilcox, one of the boys who often assisted Mr. Clackworthy in his plots against careless bank accounts.

"Holy Pet Gold Fish!" exclaimed The Early Bird. "You ain't Ashton Scott a-tall!"

"If I am I've been making an awful mistake for some forty years," Wilcox said with a laugh.

"But — but," stammered The Early Bird, pleading with Mr. Clackworthy for an explanation, "how'd Wilcox get in Ashton Scott's carriage; how'd George Bascom and Fred Little get th' jobs drivin' that outfit? How —"

"You are entitled to an explanation, James," said Mr. Clackworthy. "Ashton Scott is at this particular moment, perhaps, stepping into his carriage to start his daily trip to the office; he will arrive at his usual time of nine o'clock, and when he does —"

"But I busted up his cab."

"Oh, no, you didn't James; you just thought you did. You see I have been doing quite a business in horse-drawn vehicles of late. In addition to this ambulance, which I picked up secondhand and had repainted, I had built a replica of Ashton Scott's famous carriage.

"But it was built very, very poorly; that was the reason that it collapsed so easily when your auto struck it. A good, strong wind would have done the same thing. It was little better than a stage prop — which, in reality, it was. A little tap and our friend Wilcox was buried under a pile of twisted and broken wood.

"In his pocket he carried a thermos bottle of ox blood; that was to keep it at the right heat and prevent it congealing. At the proper moment, he gave his face a good ox-blood bath, which hid his features and made possible the delusion.

"You know we humans are great at jumping at conclusions; because it looked like Scott's carriage, it must have been Scott's carriage; because he wore a knitted shawl, it must have been Scott — that was the reasoning of those who saw the accident. It didn't occur to any one to doubt it.

"The ambulance was kept handy a few blocks away; it is this which will permit us to make our escape without detection. George Bascom and Little have already disappeared."

"But — but," sputtered The Early Bird, lost in the intricacies of the scheme, "if his nibs, th' Wheat King, ain't laid out cold, how you gonna trim him? He'll —"

"Ah, James, that's the nub of the entire matter. I sent for Scott's office manager; I whispered him the word 'Sell' — but loud enough for other traders to hear it. The office manager will follow instructions implicitly — he's been trained that way.

"By the time Ashton Scott reaches his office, within the next half hour or so, the manager will have dumped Scott's wheat into The Pit, Scott's corner will be broken, the market turned upside down beyond all hope of repair, prices dropping like the mercury in January, and the other traders picking Ashton Scott's financial bones bare."

"And you — where do you come in?" demanded The Early Bird.

"My wants are few, as Longfellow said; I margined two points with instructions to sell short when wheat dropped ten below the buying price — that will give me a hundred and twenty-five thousand dollars as the price of my trouble for dethroning a king. Our own little private war on the profiteers is progressing most satisfactorily."

"Yeah," agreed The Early Bird with a grin; he suddenly remembered one of the scenes from "Monte Cristo" which he had witnessed many years before. James raised his arm with a flourish of dramatic exaggeration and showed a pair of fingers.

"Numbah two!" he cried triumphantly, but his exuberance died a quick death.

"Say, boss, who's ever driving this outfit tap up th' old nags; I wanna get out of this thing. Y' see th' last time I was jugged, I tried to make a get-away an' th' cop biffed me over th' bean, an' — they hauled me to th' hoosgow in — in an ambulance!"

MR. CLACKWORTHY'S POT OF GOLD

Although the relaxed posture of his body suggested indolent ease as he reclined in the depths of a luxuriously comfortable, overstuffed chair, Mr. Amos Clackworthy's shrewd brain was exceedingly active. Between his eyebrows there was a faint frown, and the eyes themselves lacked that whimsical twinkle which so often accompanied the incubation of a scheme, one of those clever ideas of his, calculated to swell the Clackworthy bank balance to the corresponding diminishment of some one else's.

The truth of it was that the master confidence man's mind, while diligently in pursuit of that alluring coinage called "easy money," was only running around in circles, starting at nowhere and arriving at precisely the same place. Even a master confidence man's fund of originality must run low at times.

Occupying his favorite place by the window which looked out upon Sheridan Road, Mr. James Early, otherwise "The Early Bird," tapped the toes of his shoes soundlessly on the thick nap of the beautiful Chinese rug of blue and gold, woven together in a perfect harmony of shading. For more than an hour he had kept his peace, but not without many anxious glances toward the meditative Mr. Clackworthy.

"What's the matter, boss?" he demanded at length. "Ain'tcha able to coax an idear from the ol' bean? Mebbe if you primed the think-cylinders with a li'le joy-juice now —"

"It is the weather, James." The master confidence man sighed in admission of his discouragement. "The heat has gotten next to me, it seems." His hand reached out and tapped the card-index file, a neat little compartment of exquisitely polished rosewood matching the table; it contained the names of various men well rated financially, selected as future contributors to Mr. Clackworthy's income. There was an amazing lot of information in those brief notations, intimate data which would have surprised and dumfounded the subjects thereof; their foibles, hobbies, and, not uncommonly, the secret chapters of their lives. The rosewood file was a "prospect list," a methodical arrangement kept by the man who made the pursuit of easy money a thorough and profitable business.

"Not a single hunch," he murmured "It seems to be the closed season for my pet list of suckers, and —"

"An' it don't take no movin' van to tote the bankroll," interrupted The Early Bird quickly. "Ain't that it?" His voice took on an apprehensive inflection, but Mr. Clackworthy smiled reassuringly.

"We can hardly go into competition with the subtreasury," he admitted, "but neither are we in the imminent danger of becoming public charges. The bank balance, to speak in the concrete terms of dollars and cents, is precisely" — he turned to a penciled memo at his elbow — "nineteen thousand two hundred and sixty-three dollars thirty-three cents. In some respects a reassuring sum, but it must be remembered that a confidence man can't expect to win much confidence without a good and sufficient working capital. The sight of a neat little packet of thousand-dollar bills is more convincing than all the logic; the man who needs credit the worst has the hardest time getting it. Money is the magnate which —"

"Nix on the essay," interrupted The Early Bird ruefully; "work the chin a little less an' the noodle a little harder, boss. If the sum total of our mutual assets ain't more'n nineteen thousand two hundred an' sixty-three berries — me bein' flat, due to payin' tuition in gettin' educated to the fact that a full house ain't always worth the limit — we gotta get busy an' garner in some kale. Lately, things ain't been breakin' right for You, Us an' Company, Unincorporated."

"Yes, we've had a rotten run of luck, James," admitted Mr. Clackworthy. "If I were superstitious, perhaps I would say that an evil jinx has been dogging our footsteps."

"Huh!" snorted The Early Bird. "I hope you ain't got the notion that we've been operatin' under the guidance of a lucky star. Three flivvers out of five schemes, an' on them two we did put over you can't say that we took enough coin outta circulation to start the mint workin' overtime. I'll tell the moneyworshipin' world we didn't!"

"At least we stayed out of jail," reminded Mr. Clackworthy. "That much was lucky." The Early Bird shivered at the forced recollection of their narrow escape from durance vile; Mr. Clackworthy had played too far across the legal line and had almost come to grief.

"There was a guy what once spieled 'Money talks,'" said The Early Bird, hastily changing the subject. "I sure make the wish that it would murmur a sweet li'le lovesong into our eagerly strainin' ears; somethin' like 'I'd leave my happy home for you.' As it is, we ain't even heard it whisper."

Mr. Clackworthy laughed, his coplotter's idiomatic humor restoring his genial good nature. He reached across the table to his cigar humidor and selected one of his favorite brand of perfectos.

"That suggestion of yours, James, about appealing to Bacchus for an idea to fertilize the sterility of our brains, and —"

"What mob does this Bacchus guy train with?" demanded The Early Bird. "I ain't strong for cuttin' in no outsiders."

"My dear James!" remonstrated the master confidence man." Your ignorance of mythology is appalling. Bacchus was the legendary god of wine, and the name —"

"Aw!" grunted The Early Bird, entirely mollified. "I gotcha, boss; that was just a highbrow way, of sayin,' 'Let's wet the tonsils.' Sure, I'm on; but hereafter when you're gonna slip me an invite to a drink, it ain't necessary to be so dang fancy about it." With alacrity he touched the gong which summoned Nogo, Mr. Clackworthy's Japanese servant. James and Nogo had a sort of private code between them, and he struck four measured strokes, the signal that liquor, ice, and Seltzer were to be brought. Obedient to the summons, the smiling little Jap came in a few minutes later with a tray containing the requisite ingredients for highballs. Also he brought, tucked under his arm, the afternoon edition of the Chicago newspapers. There were four, for Mr. Clackworthy took them all and read them, from first pages to last; not even did he skip the want ads. It was not infrequently that he garnered from a chance item a bit of valuable information for his "prospect list," or even the nucleus of an idea that, under the chemistry of his mental processes, could be turned to handsome profit.

After sipping his highball, the master confidence man picked up his newspapers and began a brief but none the less thorough survey of the printed columns. For almost an hour he was so occupied when he reached page three of *The News*, the last of the daily publications to reach his attention. Without any comment to The Early Bird who, from the chair by the window was watching eagerly for any signs of a captured idea that might launch them upon a fresh adventure, Mr. Clackworthy put down the paper and lighted a fresh cigar.

Silently, absently, he smoked, meditatively and without haste; his eyelids slightly lowered; now and then he touched his long, shapely fingers to the close-cropped Vandyke beard. Presently, he stirred and reached for the decanter to mix himself another highball.

"Join me, James, and drink to the success of our latest pilgrimage in the quest of some yet unknown but carelessly tended surplus of this world's goods," he invited.

"Whatcha mean, boss?" demanded The Early Bird. "Ain'tcha got the goof picked out and numbered yet?"

"To speak in the metaphor of the shearer, my dear James," answered Mr. Clackworthy with a laugh, "we have, I think, a sharp pair of shears, but there yet remains to be found — the lamb. However, since we have the assurance of that high authority, Mr. P. T. Barnum, now deceased, that one is born every minute, I think we need entertain no fears on that score."

"Spill it!"

But the master confidence man kept his own counsel as he proceeded, between sips of his second drink, to work out various details of his yet rather embryonic scheme. After some minutes he again glanced at the third page of *The News* and then, stepping to a bookcase, he took down an atlas of the world. He turned to the map of Pennsylvania and, as The Early Bird watched him in a mounting fever of curiosity, gave studied attention to it.

"Adventure!" remarked Mr. Clackworthy, "The pot of gold at the end of the rainbow! Captain Kidd's treasure chest of pirated booty buried beneath ten feet of sand on the deserted isle! Capital!"

"Them two highballs has skyrocketed to your head, ain't

they?" demanded The Early Bird with considerable asperity. "Hanged if that chin music don't sound like you was goin' in for this free verse stuff. Ain't no sense to that lingo you're spielin'. Cut out the verbal ring-around-the-rosy an' get down to biz."

Mr. Clackworthy took a gold pencil from his vest-pocket and pressed the point of it against the dot which the Pennsylvania map makers had labeled "ALSCHOOLA" and which, from the capitals, it could be judged was a county seat. Reference to the population list, alphabetically arranged in the back of the atlas, told him that Alschoola had been censused at ten thousand souls.

"If you want to make yourself useful, James," he said, "you might start packing. We go to Alschoola, Pennsylvania, tonight; to be more exact, we start tonight. Seeing that if is some distance from the route of the through New York trains, I hazard the guess that we will arrive about day after tomorrow."

The Early Bird blinked.

"Is that on the level, boss?" he demanded. "Are we grabbin' a rattler for this burg that is pronounced with a sneeze?"

"Never more serious in my life," affirmed Mr. Clackworthy. It was to be seen that he was generating a high-voltaged enthusiasm for this new scheme, whatever it might be.

"Play the record, boss; lemme in on the know."

Mr. Clackworthy shook his head teasingly; it always amused him to see The Early Bird tortured on the rack of curiosity.

"Perhaps our liquid refreshment, James, sharpened my wits a bit; but on page three of yonder paper you will find our lead. Suppose you look it over and tell me what you think of it."

The other leaped from his chair and grabbed the copy of *The News*, but in vain did his eyes sweep up and down the columns from left to right and from right to left again, He remained as puzzled as before. True enough, there were several Associated Press dispatches from Pennsylvania, but he found none of them mentioning the town with the queer-sounding name of Alschoola. In Philadelphia, a judge had suffered a nervous breakdown as a result of trying more than a thousand divorce cases; in Pittsburgh a kidnapped boy had been returned to his broken-hearted parents.

With an impatient growl, The Early Bird threw down the paper and turned on his heel.

"Watcha goin' to this here Alschoola for?" he demanded flatly.

"Money," answered Mr. Clackworthy with unilluminating brevity.

II.

James Early did not find his first glimpse of Alschoola reassuring. As he and the master confidence man disembarked from a non-Pullman train, the only kind that operated over the twenty-five-mile branch, his first impression was that the railroad company did not care enough about Alschoola to bestow upon it a respectable passenger station. Away from the shabby depot there extended a bumpy cobblestone street, leading uphill toward the business section.

The Early Bird wasn't wildly enthusiastic about the business part of the town, either. Accusingly he swung upon the master confidence man and glared.

"I hope you ain't got no idear that we're gonna take any dough outta this place?" he demanded with disgusted skepticism. "Huh! The whole burg wouldn't auction off for fifty berries — of my jack."

"Appearances," reminded Mr. Clackworthy, "are often deceiving. And permit me to say that a town is but the composite of its strongest personalities, now and then of but one dominating personality; towns, like the men who make them, have traits of individuality. What strikes you, on the surface, as being Alschoola's outstanding trait?"

"Freezin' onto the jack," snapped The Early Bird promptly; "squeezin' down on the silver dollar until the eagle squawks an' Lady Columbia sobs for mercy."

"Right!" and Mr. Clackworthy nodded. "Step to the head of the class." He gestured toward the shabby buildings and the poorly paved, ill-lighted street ahead of them. "Here we see a miserly municipal spirit and a horror of high taxes. I think it would be a safe guess to say that Alschoola is dominated by a clique of dollar-worshiping gentlemen who find progress too expensive for their tastes. Such men, my dear James, are the sort we like to pluck."

The Early Bird grunted without enthusiasm; for himself, he preferred to have some visible evidence of the wealth that they proposed to gather in.

"When I was liftin' leathers," he said, referring to those days previous to his association with the master confidence man, "I never picked out no panhandlers when the fins was itchin' for a fat roll."

There was no station bus, the lack of a public conveyance being explained by the proximity of the hotel sign, "Alschoola House," prominently displayed half a block up the dingy street. There being, likewise, no hotel porter to lighten their burden, the two plotters had no choice but to pick up their bags and make their way hotelward.

On the corner, before reaching the hostelry, they had to pass a rusty-looking building with peelly lettering on the plate-glass window which announced: "Alschoola State Bank." Crowded up against the window was a desk before which sat a man who at the moment was fondling a packet of currency.

"See the money buzzard!" remarked The Early Bird.

Mr. Clackworthy smiled; he had to admit that there was something about the man at the bank desk, onion-smooth of pate, narrow-eyed, and with a beaked nose curving down over the upper lips of his thin mouth, which did make one think of a bird of prey.

"I wonder if that is the chief mogul of Alschoola," he said. "What a joy it would be to separate him from some of the money which he strokes so fondly!"

"Yeah," snorted The Early Bird, "an' what a joy it would be to breeze into the subtreasury some quiet P.M., an' stroll leisurely forth with a coupla suit cases full of thousand-case notes. It would be easier to take two or three million outta the mint than to bilk that bozo outta two bits."

The Alschoola House extended no cordial hand of welcome. The lazy-eyed, slow-moving clerk was smoking a corncob pipe as he watched two bearded oldsters engrossed with a game of checkers. Almost reluctantly, he tore himself away to receive the two incoming guests from Chicago.

Casting a further disapproving glance over the lobby, The Early Bird waited for Mr. Clackworthy to register. The lobby was shabbily and indifferently furnished with cane-bottomed chairs, numerous cuspidors, and a long, battered table for traveling salesmen to write their letters, at present given over to the checker game. The hotel desk itself was a counter, the top of which was covered with carpeting; at the end of it stood a fly-speckled cigar case of very doubtful-looking smokes.

"Two rooms with baths," murmured Mr. Clackworthy mechanically as he affixed his name and that of James Early to the untidy register. It was the order that he always gave for accommodations.

"Huh?" A surprised ejaculation came from the shirt-sleeved clerk, and he stared sharply, suspecting that he was being made the butt of banter.

"Two rooms and baths, if you don't mind."

"How'll a shower do?" and the clerk snickered. "Josh Duncan's rheumatism says rain, an' the roof of No. 18 is some leaky."

"Ain'tcha got no bathtubs in this joint?" demanded The Early Bird indignantly.

The clerk, perceiving that the request for baths had been quite serious, ceased grinning. He suddenly realized that Alschoola House was entertaining two guests accustomed to luxury and willing to pay for it.

"Sorry, gentlemen," he said, "but we ain't got but one bath to the floor."

Mr. Clackworthy smiled philosophically, and even offered the clerk a cigar. Past experience had shown him that considerable information of value is often to be obtained from friendly knights of the hotel desk.

"Do the best you can for us," he said cheerfully. "We shall probably be here for some time." At this prospect The Early Bird gave voice to a mournful groan and sank miserably into a chair.

The clerk was now looking the pair over in a critically appraising survey, noting the faultless tailoring of Mr. Clackworthy's one hundred-and-fifty-dollar suit, the neat cut of his Vandyke beard, the expansive opulence which exuded from his tall, impressive figure.

"You ain't — hum — sellin' stock?" he ventured suspiciously.

"No."

"It wouldn't be none of my put-in, nohow; only, if you was, I was goin' to tell you that the same train you come in on goes back in fifty minutes. This ain't no town for stock salesmen. Flint Whitecotton don't like nobody comin' in here an' packin' away Alschoola money — and what Flint Whitecotton says in this man's town, goes."

"Ah!" murmured Mr. Clackworthy, his eyes lighting with interest. "Quite the local nabob, Mr. Whitecotton."

"Yep! Owns half the town, an he's got a mortgage on the other half."

"Tell me," requested Mr. Clackworthy, "is he somewhat bald of head, with a hook-nose, and —"

"That's him, mister."

"I saw him as I passed the bank."

"Uh-huh; president of the bank. Owns the big store, flour mill, lumber yard, and —"

"An' the hotel, of course," chimed in The Early Bird from his slouched position in the chair.

"No, but I guess he will," and the clerk sighed. "He's got a mortgage on it. Like as not I'll lose my job then; we don't get along very well, Flint Whitecotton an' me. That's why I tipped you off in case you was sellin' stock. Old Flint got the city council to pass an ordinance taxin' every stock salesman a hundred dollars." He frowned, frankly puzzled; swiftly, he began checking over the list of possible businesses that might have brought the prosperous-looking gentlemen to Alschoola. Not groceries, farm implements, washing machines, patent churns — and certainly they were not book agents.

"I am an emissary of — progress," said the master confidence man.

The clerk blinked solemnly for a moment, then pounded his fist down on the carpeted top of the desk.

"You're a capitalist!" he exclaimed.

"Yes, I have been so accused."

"I ought to have guessed that right off, Mr. —" He gave a quick glance toward the register. "Mr. Clackworthy. I wonder now if you mebbe come to have a look at Whitecotton's twenty-acre tract east of town?" His tired, dreamy-looking eyes were alight now, and his voice trembled with eagerness.

Mr. Clackworthy shook his head and stated that such was not the case, but adding that he might be interested if the Whitecotton tract showed any opportunity of profit.

"It does!" the clerk cried. "There's a gold mine out there in the Whitecotton tract. If you're a capitalist, you're the man I want to talk to. There's a fortune in that deposit for them that puts it on the market. It won't take much capital."

"What sort of a deposit?"

"Statuary clay, that's what. My name's Lemuel Budkins, and you an' me ought to get together, for" — his voice raised triumphantly — "I got an option on that twenty acres of land."

It cannot be truthfully said that a deposit of sculptor's modeling clay appealed to Mr. Clackworthy as offering promise of much profit, but it did occur to him that this might, in some way or another, provide the wedge which would pry open the way into Flint Whitecotton's hoard.

"When you can spare a little time, Mr. Budkins," he said, "I'll be glad to talk things over."

"I got time right now," answered Budkins promptly; "that's all I have got." He grabbed two of the traveling bags and led the way up the hotel stairs.

A few minutes later, his forehead glistening with moisture, his eyes gleaming with the rebirth of dying hopes, he leaned forward in a chair, facing Mr. Clackworthy and The Early Bird, trying to convince them that he held the key to sudden and certain wealth.

"You see," said Mr. Budkins, "I got the idee from a feller what was boardin' down here last summer at my Aunt Mandy's. He ran across that clay deposit just by accident. Said it was the best statuary clay he ever seen. Him not havin' any capital, he let me in on it, so we organized a little company, and —"

"How much capitalization?" inquired Mr. Clackworthy.

"Oh, we ain't incorporated yet," replied Budkins. "Seems like De Vine — that's my partner's name — must have hit a snag or mebbe died or something for I ain't heard from him in most a year. I had two or three nice, encouragin' letters, an' then he quit writin' all of a sudden, but —"

"How far did you get with your promotion plans?" inquired the master confidence man.

"Not far, an' somethin' has got to be done quick, I took an option on Flint Whitecotton's twenty acres, an' it runs out on the first of the month. That's next Friday. Only paid him a hundred dollars for it, but" — he colored in embarrassment — "the truth is, Mr. Clackworthy, I ain't got any more money to pay for another option. You see, I let De Vine have four hundred dollars for his expenses, an' —"

"I gotcha," interrupted The Early Bird. "You been nicked for four hundred iron men."

Mr. Budkins looked puzzled for a moment and then flushed guiltily.

"I — I sort of begun to have that suspicion," he admitted haltingly.

"It ain't no suspicion; it's a lead-pipe cinch," said James. "Consider yourself an enrolled scholar in the School of Experience, an' a fully initiated member of The Ancient Order of Trimmed Mutts. You been buncoed, bilked, fleeced, flimflammed an' otherwise deprived of four hundred berries."

"My dear James!" reproved Mr. Clackworthy sternly. He turned apologetically to Budkins. "Have you tried to interest — ah — local capital?" he inquired politely.

"There ain't no local capital, except what Flint Whitecotton has got squeezed in them two graspin' fists of his," Budkins answered bitterly. "He ain't got no vision; can't see no further than a dollar can cast a shadow. I tried to get him interested, but he just laughed at me. I tell you, Mr. Clackworthy, it's a gold mine. Just think — thirty-five dollars a ton just for clay that can be dug off the top of the ground with a shovel. Just think of it! Easier than minin' coal, an' coal sellin' for about six dollars to the ton!"

Mr. Clackworthy could have reminded him that the consumption of sculptor's clay would total very few tons a year, that it was but an empty daydream, This, in fact, he proceeded to do, as gently and as kindly as possible.

"While I am quite certain, Mr. Budkins, that your deposit

of sculptor's clay lacks financial possibilities, I feel almost certain that I can return you the money which you would otherwise lose in the venture, and perhaps some interest besides. I shall let you know this afternoon."

Lemuel Budkins' face mirrored both disappointment and relief; it is hard, sometimes, to surrender a daydream, but five hundred dollars is a great deal of money to a man who hasn't any. In the case of the hotel clerk, the capital which had been swallowed up in his foolish, visionary scheme represented frugal economies.

When Budkins had departed, The Early Bird let his gaze wander from the cracked washbasin and pitcher on the rickety washstand in the corner of the room, to rest disgustedly on Mr. Clackworthy's face.

"Say!" he exploded. "What's the grand idear? Are we goin' around the country weedin' back some other guy's graft, or are we out to grab a little kale on our own hook?"

Mr. Clackworthy looked thoughtful for a moment.

"James," he said slowly, "during our association, have I ever taken money from a poor man? Have I ever trimmed an honest man? In my own defense, I answer, 'No!' Every man who has contributed to us, has fallen victim to his own avarice.

"The idea, my dear James, is to build a neat little trap for the local Midas known as Flint Whitecotton; a man, if my surmise is correct, as hard as his front name. The idea, my indignant partner in crime, is to convince Banker Whitecotton that he had a grievous financial mistake in optioning that twenty-acre tract of his on the edge of town."

"An' sell the option back to him, huh? What's the lay? You ain't flirtin' with the idear that you're gonna make him fall for no sculptor's clay racket?"

"Hardly!" Mr. Clackworthy laughed. "Hardly that. I fear that our hard-headed, tight-fisted banker is not so credulous as Mr. Burkin. Bestir yourself, and we shall have a look at that twenty acres of clay land."

The tract was but three miles from town, and thirty minutes later the two pursuers of easy money had made the trip in a hired flivver and were looking over the property. It was, indeed, as worthless-looking a piece of real estate as one might expect to find in the entire State of Pennsylvania. Half of it was a tangle of starved underbrush, and the remaining part of it was devoid of any growing thing, for the whitish clay was lacking in fertility. In the hot sun it was baked brick hard.

For a quarter of an hour Mr. Clackworthy devoted himself to a survey of the property, his brows knitted in thought. He noticed particularly that the State highway ran alongside the twenty acres. Although he nodded, The Early Bird's wrath grew apace.

"And now," said the master confidence man, "we will go back and proceed to take Mr. Whitecotton's measure."

"His name may be cotton," grunted James, "but I'll lay a li'le bet that you ain't gonna pick him."

"That's a sporting proposition. Any amount you like."

"A hundred seeds, boss." He cast a last disgusted glance at the desolate twenty acres and shook his head. It didn't seem humanly possible that any sane man would give up good money for it; he thought of the mysterious news item which had inspired the idea — and wondered with a curiosity which burned almost to fever heat.

III.

The building which housed the Alschoola State Bank gave no outward appearance of opulence, and neither did Mr. Flint Whitecotton, the bank's president. He wore a suit even more shabby than was the building; one judged his favorite axiom to be "A penny saved is a penny earned." The suit was frayed, threadbare, and darned in several places. The cuffs of his shirt wore aged whiskers; his shoes were unshined, as if he begrudged the cost of the polish necessary to give them a gloss; even the smoothness of his head was an item of economy. It did away with the necessity of barber bills.

Flint Whitecotton had a leathery skin, drawn drum tight over his bones. His eyes held a cold, freezing quality, and, as the bank door opened that afternoon, he frowned in black disfavor at the sinful extravagance as represented by Mr. Amos Clackworthy's perfect harmony of attire. Such sartorial prodigality, in the opinion of Mr. Whitecotton, was downright criminal.

Wasting no time in the little pleasantries generally attending a formal introduction, Mr. Clackworthy opened his wallet and put in front of the banker five bills, each of one thousand dollars' denomination. Mr. Whitecotton's eyes bulged.

"I wish to open an account," said the master confidence man crisply. "My name is Clackworthy, my home Chicago. If you desire business references —" He knew there would not be a call for them, although he could readily have supplied them; a five-thousand-dollar cash deposit speaks for itself. Worshipfully, the banker's fingers went out and began to stroke the beloved thousand-dollar bills. He gave the new depositor a look of baffled curiosity.

"Humph!" he grunted. His voice was like his face — harsh and unpleasant. "May I ask if you contemplate — ah — going into business here?"

"You might call it that."

"What line?"

"I propose to develop a resource that has been locally overlooked." Mr. Clackworthy smiled as he spoke. "If you will kindly give me credit for the five thousand, and a check book, I will write to your order a check for two thousand dollars."

"Huh? Check — two thousand — to my order?" gasped Mr. Whitecotton. He again stared at the new customer, this time as if searching for some outward signs of insanity.

"Precisely. You see, I have purchased from Lemuel Bodkins his option on that twenty acres of clay land east of town, and I wish to exercise the option. The check, if you please. You'll pardon me if I seem rather abrupt, but there are so many things I want to attend to — lumber for the buildings, some telegrams, and that sort of thing. Quite a lot of detail to getting a new enterprise started, you know."

As the banker mechanically made a notation in a pass book, an ill-concealed sneer twisted his thin lips.

"You are buying that clay land?" he demanded incredulously.

"Quite so." Already Mr. Clackworthy had uncapped his fountain pen and was filling in a check. "Just give me a receipt for it, and you can make the deed out later; tomorrow will do."

"What are you going to do with it?" demanded the banker

bluntly.

"Extract a certain chemical property valuable to science," replied the confidence man glibly; and then, with a laugh: "Oh, I assure you that it has nothing to do with sculptor's clay, Mr. Whitecotton. You would hardly expect me to be wasting my time with an insignificant scheme like Budkins'. The poor chap has had his little dream and, fortunately, gets out with a whole skin and a little to spare. I gave him seven hundred dollars for his option."

"What?" The banker's tone rose to a shrill note for two reasons. One was because it seemed such an unnecessary waste of money — seven hundred dollars tossed away to a visionary young fool like Lem Budkins, when a hundred would have done quite as well; the other was that the option would have expired within another week. This extravagantly dressed stranger evidently wanted the twenty acres badly, and how Flint Whitecotton would have made him pay!

"Sure," said Mr. Clackworthy. "I felt sorry for the chap." The banker shivered; such costly pity was beyond his ken. Immediately he formed a very low regard for Mr. Clackworthy's ability as a business man.

IV.

Within the succeeding days, Alschoola was shown some speed. A neat but inexpensive shack went up on the Whitecotton twenty acres, almost overnight. Mr. Clackworthy paid spot cash for the lumber and the carpenter hire. The town, of course, was abuzz with speculation and guesses; but no one except Mr. Clackworthy knew, and he didn't tell. Even The Early Bird was not, as he would say, "in on the know," a fact which galled him bitterly.

With the completing of the shack and a high board fence, total cost eight hundred dollars, the two mysterious strangers began to keep regular hours, admitting no one. The town wondered what they did there, and would have been further mystified to have witnessed the strange capitalist calmly stretched out in a steamer chair, reading a volume of Freud's *Psychoanalysis*, while The Early Bird paced the floor like a caged lion, smoking countless cigarettes and muttering angrily.

It was midafternoon and James gave way to his daily explosion.

"I gotta have a look-in!" he stormed. "You gotta tell me what the lay is."

Mr. Clackworthy looked up lazily.

"We are going to sell Mr. Whitecotton's worthless farm back to him — at a handsome profit," he answered innocently. "I thought you knew that."

"But how are you gonna hook him?" demanded The Early Bird. "What's the bait we're usin'?"

"Gold," answered Mr. Clackworthy solemnly, "a pot of gold. Didn't you read that item on the third page of —"

"I didn't see nothin' from no Pennsylvania towns except —"

"As it happens," interrupted Mr. Clackworthy with a chuckle, "it wasn't a news item from any Pennsylvania town, but an Associated Press dispatch from Washington, D. C., relating to a certain Congressional inquiry which is now in progress and occupying generous amounts of space almost daily. Question me no further, James; this is a little guessing contest of mine. Try your luck at it."

"You know I ain't got a chance."

"Very well, I'll add a bit more," said Mr. Clackworthy, "Our mutual friend and often able assistant, George Bascom, will arrive in Alschoola day after tomorrow. He will remain entire stranger to both of us. We've never seen him before; we don't know him from Adam's off-ox.

"George will appear in Alschoola garbed in tatters which will make a Russian refugee look like Beau Brummel. He is empty of pocket and desperate of mind; he appeals to Banker Whitecotton. Mr. Whitecotton is skeptical and at the same time credulous. He doesn't believe George's story, but it has such a ring of truth, backed up by such a wealth of newspaper accounts, that he dare not ignore the chance of finding out if it is really true that his clay land is worth, not a mere two thousand dollars, but a hundred times that sum."

"Two hundred thousand smackers?" gasped The Early Bird.

"Your multiplication is correct," and Mr. Clackworthy

nodded. "Mr. Whitecotton will be half convinced that his clay farm is worth two hundred thousand dollars in cash. And, on the evening of the day after tomorrow, George will proceed to convince him entirely — by a personally conducted visit to this very spot. Does it now become clear to you, my dear James?"

"Huh! Just as clear, boss, as a cloudy day on Lake Mich," The Early Bird remarked, then groaned. "Come on an' gimme a look-in."

Mr. Clackworthy shook his head teasingly and glanced at his watch.

"Come to think about it," he murmured, "I'll have to be getting to the bank for a little talk with Mr. Whitecotton. He's got a sight draft on me for thirty-two hundred dollars, and I've only eighteen hundred on deposit to meet it."

"Whatcha talkin' about? Ain'tcha got five thousand iron men in your kick?"

"True enough," said the master confidence man, "but what is in my pocket is not for Mr. Whitecotton to know. He is to be only aware that of the five thousand dollars I deposited in his bank, just one thousand eight hundred dollars remain. And — I don't want to meet the draft, anyhow. It's one that Pop Blanchard sent here; just a little touch in realism."

Half an hour later, Mr. Clackworthy, not looking so cheerful as he inwardly felt, was closeted with the local banker. Almost accusingly, Mr. Whitecotton produced the sight draft, a demand that one Mr. Amos Clackworthy pay over the sum of three thousand two hundred dollars forthwith.

"What about this?" he demanded.

"It's for some machinery that I have ordered, and which won't be shipped until it is paid," said Mr. Clackworthy with apparent glumness. "I need that machinery, and I need it bad. I can't get started until I have it; things haven't gone as smoothly as I had anticipated, and I hope that you —"

"There is but one question before me," cut in the banker icily. "Have you the money to meet this draft, or shall I sent it back unpaid?"

"You've got to help me out, Mr. Whitecotton," pleaded Mr. Clackworthy, "I've got a balance of one thousand eight hundred dollars on deposit; I need one thousand four hundred dollars to meet the draft. I paid you two thousand dollars for the land; suppose you lend me one thousand four hundred dollars on a ten-day note, with the land as security."

Banker Whitecotton laughed shrilly.

"Lend you one thousand four hundred dollars on that pile of clay?" he snorted. "It isn't worth fifty dollars an acre. I wouldn't give you thirty dollars an acre for it."

"But I paid you a hundred an acre."

"A bargain is a bargain," retorted the banker. "No one asked you to buy that land from me. Don't argue; I won't lend you a dollar on your hare-brained scheme."

"That's because you don't understand the chemical possibilities," persisted Mr. Clackworthy with just as much earnestness as if he had really expected to win the man over. He launched into a long, apparently technical, explanation of his contemplated process of extracting certain expensive chemicals from that peculiar whitish loam — all of which was Greek to the Alschoola banker.

"See here, Mr. Whitecotton," he went on, "I stand on the brink of success or failure. There has been a slight hitch in my plans; the money I expect to get has not come into my hands yet. I hope —"

"So did half-witted Lem Budkins," snapped Whitecotton.

"Take a look at this," pleaded Mr. Clackworthy, producing a letter. It was ostensibly from a New York chemical company offering him twenty thousand dollars for his entire rights. The banker, of course, had no way of knowing that those letterheads had been printed on Mr. Clackworthy's order and mailed by Pop Blanchard in New York; nevertheless, he tossed it aside with hardly a glance.

"Not interested," he said harshly. "You haven't the money to pay the draft; therefore, I send it back."

"And force me to sell out for a paltry twenty thousand dollars!" Mr. Clackworthy exclaimed bitterly. Mr. Whitecotton winced; it hurt him to hear such a sum sneeringly referred to as "paltry."

V.

The following afternoon, on the five o'clock train, George

Bascom arrived in Alschoola. According to previous instructions, he was shabbily dressed, wore a dented derby hat, and had a four-day bristle of beard on his normally round and clean-shaven face.

He slouched almost furtively up the street away from the railroad station. The bank, of course, was closed, but he made inquiries at Hope's Drug Store and had himself directed to the residence of Flint Whitecotton. The banker was on the front porch of his cottage — it, like everything else he owned, had been secured with the smallest possible outlay of cash — fanning himself with a palm-leaf fan, which was an advertisement and had cost him nothing, waiting for supper. He glared at the approach of the ragged stranger.

"Go away!" he called. "We don't feed tramps."

"Mr. Whitecotton," said George. "I'm no tramp, and you've got to listen to me. I'm a chauffeur, and —"

"Save your breath; I don't need a chauffeur. I haven't any automobile — not with gasoline at thirty cents a gallon. Sinful extravagance, that is!"

"I don't want a job, either," went on George Bascom; "I don't want money or free food or a job. All I want is that you should listen to me."

"Well, so long as it don't cost anything," agreed Banker Whitecotton a little less grudgingly, "I'll listen."

"To keep you from throwing me off the place for a lunatic," began George, "I'll show you some of these newspaper clippings." He poked a grimy hand into his pocket and brought out a half dozen badly worn newspaper clippings. "Just glance over those, and then I'll talk."

Flint Whitecotton did glance them over, and his impatience gave way to curiosity.

"Well?" he demanded.

"Maybe you wonder why I come to you," went on George. "I'll tell you why. It's because I'm too dead broke to buy so much as a shovel to dig for the gold that is buried — I won't tell you where until we make a deal. Any minute I'm liable to be arrested as a vagrant. Your city marshal followed me three blocks when I got off the train. Two hundred thousand dollars in gold weighs a lot more than any one man can pack. There's got to be a car to take it away. Understand? I've got to have help. Sure, I might have gone in with some crook, but he'd probably have knifed me in the back for my share.

"If I tell you where it's buried, do we split fifty-fifty? There's only two people on earth who know where it's hid, me and the woman, and she don't dare to make a move, on account of the government agents watching her so close. Do we make a deal?"

There was a light of fascination in Flint Whitecotton's cold, blue eyes; as Mr. Clackworthy had predicted, he could hardly believe it, and yet he dared not doubt it entirely. There was just one thing that decided him — no expense was involved.

"I'll go in with you," he agreed, "I'll buy the shovels. We don't have to go to the cost of hiring an automobile until we're sure it's where you say it was buried. Where is that place?"

"On your own land," answered George Bascom, "that patch of yours out on the State road. It's buried four feet down in the clay. I can take you right to the spot; I'll take you now."

A hoarse cry burst through the lips of the miserly banker. The land that he had sold for two thousand dollars was worth almost a quarter of a million dollars in buried treasure!

VI.

Even Mr. Clackworthy in his most confident moments had not anticipated that things would go through to such a whirlwind finish. He had not dreamed that the banker's greed would be so sharply whetted that he would plunge in, head over heels, within a few hours. The reason for it, no doubt, was Whitecotton's fear that George Bascom, to all appearances the penniless, desperate possessor of a two-hundred-thousand dollar secret, would discover that he, the banker, was no longer the owner of the treasure-bearing twenty acres. George, too, must have told his story well and convincingly for the cautious, canny miser to have swallowed it, hook, line, and sinker.

But that is just what happened, and Mr. Clackworthy, who had planned many further elaborate details, was totally unprepared to receive a summons from Flint Whitecotton the next morning.

"Mr. Clackworthy," began the banker, "perhaps I was — um — rather hasty with you during our last talk. However, I have — ah — been thinking it over, and I have decided that I owe it as my duty as a — ah — a public-spirited citizen to take an interest in this budding enterprise of yours. That letter you showed to me, in which you were offered twenty thousand dollars to sell out — that in itself shows that your venture must have merit."

Mr. Clackworthy looked discouraged.

"I was just on the verge of sending a wire to the New York firm, telling them that I would accept twenty-five thousand dollars and get out. They expected, of course, to raise the ante when they offered twenty thousand dollars. The truth of it is, Mr. Whitecotton, that I'm too small a fellow to fight the big combine; that's what scared off the capital that had been promised me. My hands are up; I quit. There's no use in talking things over; I'm going to sell out."

"I wouldn't do that," interposed Banker Whitecotton hastily. "Now why can't we form a company? Perhaps I would put up ten thousand dollars, but — um — I would, of course, expect to control."

"I'd rather sell out than be frozen out later," retorted Mr. Clackworthy shrewdly. "No, so long as I'm whipped, I'll take all the money I can get." He started to get from his chair, but the banker stopped him insistently. They talked for two long, haggling hours, and at length, cold sweat pouring from his bald forehead, Flint Whitecotton, the stingiest man whom Amos Clackworthy had ever done business with, inclined his head slowly, reluctantly; he agreed to give twenty-five thousand dollars.

Again Mr. Clackworthy and The Early Bird were passengers on the non-Pullman train on the branch line which terminated at Alschoola. This time, however, they were bound away from the shabby, unprogressive town, for which James was thankful; within the wallet of the master confidence man reposed twenty-five thousand dollars in currency, and for this they were both thankful.

But The Early Bird's forehead was corrugated with a

puzzled frown.

"I ain't got it all through the old bean yet, boss," he admitted. "You're tryin' to tell me that the old dollar squeezer come across with twenty-five thousand smackers because he swallowed George Bascom's fairy tale about there bein' a coupla hundred thousand in the yellow stuff in the terra firma of that clay farm you bought off'n him for a coupla thousand berries?"

"It was realism, that did the trick, my dear James," said Mr. Clackworthy, chuckling. "That, and his naturally greedy, grasping nature. Moreover, he thought he was playing safe so far as his twenty-five thousand is concerned. Before he closed with me, he sent a wire to The Gotham Chemical Corporation, asking them if they would give twenty-five thousand dollars to buy me out; since The Gotham Chemical Corporation is Pop Blanchard, the answer was 'Yes.'

"He didn't suspect a flimflam, because he couldn't imagine any sane man who would risk paying out two thousand dollars on a long chance."

"What I'm gettin' at, boss," said The Early Bird, "is, what was the hocus-pocus that made him fall for George Bascom's fake about that buried gold?"

"You're hopeless," and Mr. Clackworthy sighed. "You read the newspapers every day, too. Certainly you should recall that for some time there has been a Congressional inquiry regarding a certain war slacker named Grover Blindhouse, who escaped from army imprisonment and made his way to Europe. The Congressional inquiry brought out that the young man's mother, the widow of a wealthy Pennsylvania brewer, got together the astounding sum of two hundred thousand dollars in cash and buried it not many miles from Philadelphia for her son's use in his flight. However, the money is still buried; she dare not try to recover it, for fear that secret-service agents will shadow her and the government confiscate it, and she won't tell where it was buried. The clipping which gave me the inspiration for this very profitable adventure of ours —"

He paused and reached into his pocket. The Early Bird accepted the scrap of paper and read:

SEEK BLINDHOUSE
CHAUFFEUR WHO DROVE
$200,000 TREASURE CAR

Congressional Inquiry Reveals Name of
Man Who Can Lead Way
to Buried Wealth.

"I gotcha, boss!" exclaimed The Early Bird "George Bascom slipped Whitecotton a yarn about bein' the missin' chauffeur."

"As a finishing touch," continued Mr. Clackworthy, "I've given the old miser something to puzzle about. At the spot where he will dig, there is planted an iron chest containing — a hundred dollars in pennies. And that's your money, by the way, James."

"But," said The Early Bird with an apprehensive shudder, "that bird is gonna be some wild — if he don't drop dead on the spot. What if he starts investigatin' an' finds that fake chemical company —"

"Checkmate!" exclaimed Mr. Clackworthy. "The only way he can get us convicted, my dear James, is to plead guilty himself to a conspiracy against the government. We have got him, as they say, going and coming."